It was the sheer proximity of Julius, his strength, his size, the seductive flash of his smile

She wanted him.

It had begun before the kiss, but after, there was no denying her desire. She grew fascinated with him. The width of his hands, the thickness of his fingers, the sturdy curve of his shoulder. She would gaze too long at his face, the blue eyes that always startled her, the broad cheekbones, the hard chin, until he slowly swung his gaze to her. Even then, she'd last only three seconds more before she looked away, leaving him amused.

She was fascinated by him.

She'd sit past dark and think of Julius. He'd taught her all the things she needed to learn on the farm, but she decided, she would ask him to teach her one more lesson....

Dear Reader,

Welcome to Harlequin American Romance, where our goal is to give you hours of unbeatable reading pleasure.

Kick starting the month is another enthralling installment of THE CARRADIGNES: AMERICAN ROYALTY continuity series. In Michele Dunaway's *The Simply Scandalous Princess*, rumors of a tryst between Princess Lucia Carradigne and a sexy older man leads to the king issuing a royal marriage decree! Follow the series next month in Harlequin Intrigue.

Another terrific romance from Pamela Browning is in store for you with *Rancher's Double Dilemma*. When single dad Garth Colquitt took one look at his new nanny's adorable baby girl, he knew there had to be some kind of crazy mix-up, because his daughter and her daughter were twins! Was a marriage of convenience the solution? Next, don't miss *Help Wanted: Husband?* by Darlene Scarlera. When a single mother-to-be hires a handsome ranch hand, she only has business on her mind. Yet, before long, she wonders if he was just the man she needed—to heal her heart. And rounding out the month is Leah Vale's irresistible debut novel *The Rich Man's Baby*, in which a dashing tycoon discovers he has a son, but the proud mother of his child refuses to let him claim them for his own…unless love enters the equation.

This month, and every month, come home to Harlequin American Romance—and enjoy!

Best,

Melissa Jeglinski
Associate Senior Editor
Harlequin American Romance

HELP WANTED: HUSBAND?

Darlene Scalera

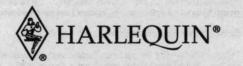

HARLEQUIN®

TORONTO • NEW YORK • LONDON
AMSTERDAM • PARIS • SYDNEY • HAMBURG
STOCKHOLM • ATHENS • TOKYO • MILAN • MADRID
PRAGUE • WARSAW • BUDAPEST • AUCKLAND

ISBN 0-373-16923-X

HELP WANTED: HUSBAND?

This edition published by arrangement with Harlequin Books S.A.

® and TM are trademarks of the publisher. Trademarks indicated with ® are registered in the United States Patent and Trademark Office, the Canadian Trade Marks Office and in other countries.

Visit us at www.eHarlequin.com

Printed in U.S.A.

ABOUT THE AUTHOR

Darlene Scalera is a native New Yorker who graduated magna cum laude from Syracuse University with a degree in public communications. She worked in a variety of fields, including telecommunications and public relations, before devoting herself full-time to romance fiction writing. She was instrumental in forming the Saratoga, New York, chapter of Romance Writers of America and is a frequent speaker on romance writing at local schools, libraries, writing groups and women's organizations. She currently lives happily ever after in upstate New York with her husband, Jim, and their two children, J.J. and Ariana. You can write to Darlene at P.O. Box 217, Niverville, NY 12130.

Books by Darlene Scalera

HARLEQUIN AMERICAN ROMANCE

Don't miss any of our special offers. Write to us at the following address for information on our newest releases.

Harlequin Reader Service
U.S.: 3010 Walden Ave., P.O. Box 1325, Buffalo, NY 14269
Canadian: P.O. Box 609, Fort Erie, Ont. L2A 5X3

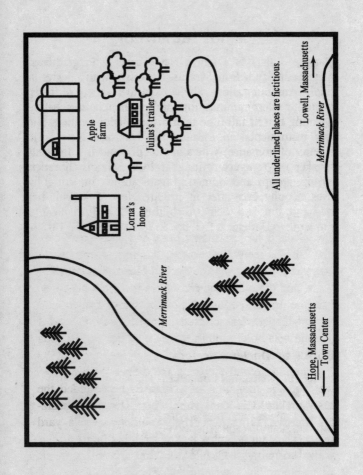

Apple farm

Julius's trailer

Lorna's home

Merrimack River

Hope, Massachusetts
Town Center

Merrimack River

Lowell, Massachusetts

All underlined places are fictitious.

Chapter One

He was the largest man Lorna had ever seen. Not that she'd seen that many, having spent three-quarters of her life at the Sacred Heart Academy for Girls, and the other quarter within these county lines. But she'd seen enough. One too many, the population of Hope, Massachusetts, was still saying, and if anyone was bold enough to say it to her face, Lorna would have to agree.

Standing behind the trees she'd been pruning, she watched the mountain of a man as he rounded the rusty pickup. His jeans were worn white, emphasizing sturdy Viking legs. His shoulders were a yard wide. The faded denim jacket stretched across their width normally would be too thin for this time of year, but today's weather was good. Only the old snow in the woods remembered winter. The man crossed onto her property and with each heavy step, she waited for the ground to give a fine tremble.

He stopped, his gaze on her house. It was an upright saltbox, formerly New England austere until five days ago when Lorna had found some old shutters in the shed and painted them yellow. Not a polite yellow. A screaming yellow. She suspected it was this trimming that held the stranger's eye. She was going to paint the weathered door next. Blue—a brilliant, peacock-strutting blue. No more somber colors. That was one thing she'd sworn off when she'd buried her husband less than six weeks ago. Life was too short and too brazen for grim colors. Good to her new vow, she'd worn chartreuse to the funeral. She'd sashayed past the pews, the murmurs soft as pillow talk. Still Lorna knew what they whispered. *A madness born from grief.* Craziness was expected, even excused, when two days earlier your husband had been surprised by a shotgun while in bed with another man's wife and shot in an area of the anatomy unmentionable in mixed company. Suffice it to say, the tale would never be told without men wincing and women nodding in silent satisfaction that God does indeed work in mysterious ways.

But there'd been no madness for Lorna that day her philandering husband was laid to his eternal rest. If she'd ever been crazy, it was three months before when she'd actually believed her husband had married her for love instead of her family's money. No, that day as she'd moved past the murmuring congregation, her clarity was as vivid as the casket's polished brass.

She had made her way down the aisle, squinting at her father already in the front pew, which had always belonged to McDonoughs. Her ancestors had founded Hope, each generation adding acquisitions and properties until today, the family was the richest in the county and its head, Axel McDonough, known to one and all—even his only daughter—as simply "the Boss."

But that day, as her father had turned to his daughter coming up the aisle, she'd seen the always-present disapproval on his face deeper than the ruts still frozen in the road. And in that moment, sashaying in her chartreuse A-line, with her wonderful clearheadedness, Lorna had known she would never call him or any man "the Boss" again.

The giant hadn't moved. Lorna levered her arm, testing the weight of the hand cutters. Without a doubt, the stranger had the meat and the muscle, but she had her newly earned lucidity. No man would ever get the best of her again.

The stranger staring at the house suddenly smiled, releasing the years from his face, adding devilish lights. Lorna locked her knees, the pad of her index finger testing the pruners' pointed tips. She'd seen smiles come easily like that before.

HOPE, JULIUS HOLT thought. It was the town's name. It was also what had brought him here. He liked it— the name—and that was good enough reason as any for a man with no patience for self-examination. He'd seen the Help Wanted ad and followed the road that shadowed the river's path to the south, the route so curved he could only see to the next bend and then no farther. He'd seen the fields first, then the orchard stretching to the sky's line. Many of the trees had been let go too long. Their branches were tangled or reached wide, shivering in the slight breeze, but light showed between the stripped limbs, and their rows were neat and even. He'd let the thick-trunked trees lead him, imagining a farmhouse at their end so old and settled no windows opened without a wrestle. The outside could probably use paint, but snow crocuses would be coming through the moist soil and lilac bushes would soon bud to soften the house's plain corners. And beneath that shingled roof, there would be a family, a dog that rarely barked and a million memories. Julius had followed the long road, the gray trees to his right and the river too far in the distance to hear its flow, and imagined that house as clearly as he knew no hard-living man such as himself belonged there. Then he'd rounded a curve and been stopped cold by those canary-yellow shutters as out of place as he'd been his whole life. He'd pulled over to the side, gotten out, taken only a few steps when those brassy shutters stopped him once more. He'd smiled and thought, *Well, I'll be damned. Hope.*

He was at the orchard's edge when a sharp green

streak flashed between all that gray. A thin, tall woman stepped out from the angled rows in a vivid lime sweatsuit completely at odds with her pinched lips and her brow's stern set. It was another sight so unexpected his smile came back wider. He stood, grinning ear to ear, knowing he looked as idiotic as the rail of a woman draped in Mardi Gras colors and aiming the pruners' steel points at his heart.

"Ma'am." He nodded.

"It's 'miss,'" she corrected, her superior tone harsh to his ears.

"Miss," he obliged. He reached into his back pocket, she all the time eyeing him, her grip strong on the cutters. He pulled out a torn piece of newspaper, unfolded it. "I've come about the job."

Her eyes narrowed to inspect him. He kept his gaze steady and waited for her to speak. Her eyes were the gray-green of a river and soft as the rest of her seemed hard. She blinked fast. Her eyes narrowed even further. She pressed a hand to her stomach and raised her other arm, brushing it across her brow's high slope, pointing the cutters heavenward. She blinked hard. Her expression shifted. He saw the surprise in her features such as he'd felt moments ago. Her arm dropped. The cutters hit the ground. The woman swayed like the spare, overgrown limbs behind them.

"Ma'am...I mean, miss..."

He looked into her eyes. Helplessness came into

the gray-green waters as the woman whispered in a most confounding feminine plea, "Oh, my," and keeled over onto his feet.

"Miss? Miss?" Julius squatted and shook the woman's shoulder. Her eyes stayed closed, but she seemed to be breathing. He shook her shoulder harder. "C'mon, lady, don't leave me now," he heard himself plead as if he'd been searching his whole life for a carnival-colored, run-down farm with a mistress to match. He picked up her sharp-boned wrist, grateful for the faint but steady pulse beneath his fingertips. He patted the back of her hand, glancing around. Even if he was the type to yell for help, there didn't seem to be another soul about the place. He looked down at the long-boned woman. Her face, relieved of expression, had lost its stern lines. Her skin was clear and smooth as the day's rise.

He checked again but saw no one. "Damn." He gathered the woman in his arms and lifted her.

LORNA WAS FLOATING, the gentle, rocking motion and pleasant solid warmth too agreeable to give up. She cracked her eyes, stared at a gold glint just beyond her nose, focusing until a saintly face became recognizable. She reached to touch the shining face.

"Saint Nicholas."

She snapped her head back. Past a thick neck, the gold image suspended on a chain around it, she saw the man. His full lips were dry and naturally curved as if always amused. His eyes were a startling hot blue, the exact shade she'd envisioned painting the front door. The color caught and held her.

"Patron saint of—"

She heard no more, twisting like a wild animal in the powerful arms around her. Her hands flailed at the man's face. "Let me go."

"Easy now," the man said, with such an note of tenderness she was startled into a second of submission. The beat of his heart was beside her ear. The rhythm matched each step he took. She arched her body and thrashed once more.

"There now." Even as her hands struck at him, caught him square on his jaw, he eased her onto the porch steps with the same surprising gentleness she'd heard in his voice. He stepped back, not even bothering to rub his chin where her blows had landed. He looked down at her with his always-amused expression. Her chest heaving from the fight still boiling within her, she glared at him, gathering details for the police report. His features were strong, blunt, like stone whose lines had been gradually worn by the elements. His eyebrows were thick, black and heavy, emphasizing the lightning blue of his eyes. She could still feel his arms around her.

"You might better sit a moment or two. You went down like a sack of potatoes, miss."

"I fainted?" she asked, though now she remembered the dizzying wave, the light-headedness that often came when she rose too fast or forgot to eat. Her anger lessened as quickly as it'd been ignited. She sucked in her cheeks and looked away, her irritation only at herself. She felt like a fool. "I skipped breakfast." Actually she'd tried a few saltines but hadn't been able to keep them down. She glanced at her watch. "And lunch."

She pushed herself off the steps.

"You should sit."

"Thank you, I'm fine." She ran her hand across her crown, checking for loose strands as she drew herself up. "Thank you for your help."

The man's hands reached out to steady her. She stared at those large wide hands, remembering their strength. She raised her head, met those brilliant blue eyes. She made her voice all business. "You're interested in the position?"

He studied her. She was taller than an average woman and long limbed, long fingered. Her face was long, too, and her lips full but pressed fast to each other. Her nostrils were cut high. Her gray-green eyes were flat as smoke now but closed, their lids were milk-white and fine veined as lace. And when they'd first opened, as he'd carried her in his arms, those eyes had held the sweetness men oftentimes thought about at night.

Those eyes focused on him now with the sober stare of a taskmaster. Turn and run, he thought, self-preservation his first instinct. But behind the woman, he saw those wild yellow shutters, proclaiming their right to be. "Yes, Miss—"

She brushed her hand once more across her smooth crown, looked tired. "It's Mrs., truth be told."

She felt the dizziness come again as his blue eyes examined her. She reached for the porch rail, but when his eyes darkened with concern, she straightened and stood without support. "Mrs. O'Reilly."

"Mrs. O'Reilly." He considered her a mute moment, then smiled. She saw in that smile a man used to finding favor with women. "If I might speak to the boss?"

Her long frame became even taller. "You're speaking to the boss, Mr....?"

The surprise in his eyes stayed only a breath, but the smile remained, his face full of a warmth and invitation that made most women instinctively lower their lashes as they returned his smile. Lorna pinched her lips together.

"Holt. Julius Holt, Mrs. O'Reilly."

She folded her arms across her chest and spoke through tight lips. "Had much experience, Mr. Holt?"

He smiled still. "More than most."

Her lips pursed, her earlier vexation gaining strength again. "How about at farming, Mr. Holt?"

"Born to it, ma'am, in Oklahoma on my granddaddy's farm until it went bust and my father moved us to California to try our luck there. I was about seven I recall.''

His tone had turned conversational, as if ready to tell her anything she wanted to hear.

''And did you have any?''

''Ma'am?''

''Luck? Did you and your family have any luck in California?''

He shook his head, the easygoing smile joined by a dry chuckle. ''Not a speck.'' His face sobered. ''We were living in an old boxcar set on concrete blocks when my daddy had a cerebral hemorrhage.'' He leaned in, the laughter gone and those blue eyes electric. ''Dead.'' He snapped his fingers. Lorna jumped. ''Right before my eyes. Just like that.'' He leaned back. ''The biggest surprise was the drink didn't get him first. Ma hung on for a while, raised chickens, had a big garden, but eventually the drink did take her.'' His delivery became matter-of-fact. ''I worked the farms in the valley beside the Mexicans almost a year before the State caught up to my sister and me.''

''How old were you?'' She hadn't meant for the question to come out so soft.

''Thirteen.''

''Thirteen?'' Lorna tipped her head, eyeing him. She'd heard lies before.

He leaned in too close again. He knew she wanted

to step back, but she didn't. He liked that in her. "By twelve, I could buck hay all day."

The woman raised her chin, the high flare of her nostrils giving her a haughty expression that instinctively provoked him. He tilted his own head, about to give her the old once-over when he noticed the garish green of her outfit again. His belligerence slid away to amused appreciation again for this odd woman with a penchant for outlandish colors. He let his grin widen, wearing it as boldly as her flamboyant colors, knowing both their affections were only to deflect focus.

He looked around, casual-like, assessing the farm instead of the woman. Past the set of her shoulders, he saw the buildings, one so dilapidated he wondered why winter winds hadn't taken it out of its misery. The others needed repair also. He saw stretches of tarpaper where shingles once had been. An old car with no wheels sat rusting beside one low-roofed building. A door hung by one hinge off another. Farther on, he saw fallen trees flattening the brambled remains of plantings. Enough work here for an army of men, let alone one man who never seemed to stay a month or two before circumstances or need drove him on.

Still he had to admire that orchard with its bull-necked trunks stretching out in every direction. Real pretty country once he'd gotten past the new subdivisions beginning to surround the main part of town.

He saw the pond in the lower field thawing at its edges, looked to the slopes of the land resting at the horizon. A man could sit, take a breath and feel whole here. Julius's gaze moved back to the tight-mouthed woman. His pleasure receded. Pretty land and loud colors aside, the schoolmarm and he weren't exactly a match made in heaven. He met her snooty expression and the urge to needle her arose as naturally as the smile still on his face.

"The ad said starting salary was seven dollars an hour?"

She nodded. "Plus room and board."

"Seven dollars an hour?" He was incredulous. He didn't think it was possible, but her mouth pinched even tighter. He was enjoying himself now.

"It's a reasonable wage."

He let out a laugh. "It's an allowance, sister."

She squared her shoulders. His gaze dropped as her nicely shaped breasts thrust up.

"I am not your—" Her lean, long frame weaved as if to fold up on itself once more.

"Whoa." He caught her elbow, moved beside her and supported her lower back with his other hand. "No law says we can't sit while we negotiate, is there now?"

Her body tensed beneath his touch. She shook him off, easing herself onto the steps without his help. He saw the fine flush of sweat across that high, proud brow. He patted his pants pocket, hoping for a tissue.

One pocket was empty except for a worn wallet with no pictures and little money. In the other pocket, he found a cocktail napkin with a name and telephone number that he'd never call scrawled across it. He shoved the napkin at the woman.

She glanced down at the wrinkled square he thrust at her.

"The Fat Dog Grille" was imprinted in a curve across its top. Beneath it, the name and number were written in a feminine flourish. The woman looked up at Julius. "Lulu? You actually know someone named Lulu?"

He smiled slowly. "And she's not even the first Lulu I've known…nor the last, God willing."

She snatched the napkin from him, her gaze stern even as she tucked her lip as if biting back a smile. She paled and pressed the square to cheek. She flattened her hand against her stomach.

"You gonna be sick?" His alarm was real.

The woman took a deep breath and sat up yet straighter, which until then, Julius hadn't thought possible. Her spine stiff and her expression inflexible, she handed him back the napkin. "There is no negotiation, Mr. Holt. The pay is, as stated, seven dollars an hour with room and board."

Pursing his lips in imitation of the woman, he studied the acreage as if actually considering her offer.

"You put up those shutters?" He glanced away from the bright rectangles quickly, catching her off guard, her expression unschooled. He didn't want to see what he saw. He knew she didn't want him to see it either—the flash of desperation. His impulsive smile disappeared. Those gray-green eyes were going to be her undoing. His, too.

He was about to say goodbye when he saw a keen challenge in her gaze.

"Don't change the subject, Mr. Holt."

He sat on the steps, spread his knees so his body took up more space. He plucked a piece of grass. "Are you offering me the job, Mrs. O'Reilly?"

She inched to the opposite side of the steps. "No."

"So, negotiations are still open?"

"No, Mr. Holt. There are no negotiations." She stood too quickly, grasped the rail. He reached for her arm but she twisted away from him, steadied herself on the rail.

"Liver," he said.

"I beg your pardon?" She swiveled her head toward him; her eyes gradually refocused to find him.

"Eat some liver. It's full of iron." He took in her slim frame. Her legs were long as a restless night. "You take a multivitamin?"

She folded her hands at her waist. "Thank you for your concern, Mr. Holt, but I'll be fine. Thank you for coming by."

He'd been dismissed, but only his gaze moved to his pickup on the shoulder of the dirt road, then back at the woman with her neon-green sweatshirt and her crazy yellow shutters and her colorless face. "Had a lot of others apply for the job?"

"You're the first."

He liked her for not lying. He smiled. She sank onto the steps as if even her slight weight was suddenly too much.

"Yes," she said.

"Yes?"

"I painted those shutters."

He kept smiling at her. "It's a fine yellow."

Her expression stayed tense except those betraying gray-green eyes softened. "Soon as I get a chance, the door's going to be bright blue."

He studied the weathered door, nodding as if he could already see it painted. "You like bright colors?"

"Never much thought about it until I wore chartreuse to my husband's funeral last month." She shrugged, looked tired. "Now I can't seem to get enough of them."

"I'm sorry."

She looked at him as if she didn't understand. "About your husband," he clarified.

"Oh." She looked out to the road.

Her reaction intrigued him. "You're not?" Instinctively he knew she wouldn't lie.

She looked at him. "I wasn't happy about it, mind you."

He was silent but not in judgment. He'd also known men who had deserved to die. He didn't ask what happened. He had no right. Still, if she decided to tell him, he would listen. Everyone deserved that much. He plucked a piece of grass, traced its length and gave her silence should she want to speak.

She watched him from the corner of her eyes, liking the quiet, thoughtful way he touched the grass as if it were priceless.

"He was in bed with another man's wife," she said flatly. "The husband found them. They called it a crime of passion. Passion." She repeated the word and shook her head.

He saw her eyes confused and vulnerable and, without a doubt, a man's undoing.

He shifted on the step, his hand reaching to tug at the bill of his baseball cap before he remembered he'd taken it off in the truck. He liked to face a new situation bareheaded, barefaced, without his eyes shaded, signaling secrets. Not that he wasn't like everyone else with one or two hidden truths. He couldn't help wondering what mysteries the woman beside him concealed?

He shifted again. The woman stared at the dirt road as if waiting for an answer to come walking down its dusty length. The silence stretched out.

"The woman with your husband?" He broke the silence.

She turned to him, her expression sharp.

"Her name wasn't Lulu, was it?"

Like a traitor, one corner of her mouth crept up, then the other followed. He knew she didn't want to but she smiled, everything about her softening, and he knew her laughter would sound pretty to a man's ears. Her eyes gentled again, as if grateful. She brushed her hand across her crown, although not one hair dared stray from the ponytail low on her neck. He had to leave. A vulnerable widow with shrimp-pink lips and gray-green eyes that turned warm when she smiled. Seven dollars an hour. He'd been wrong about those shutters or he would have heeded their warning as soon as he saw that neon yellow. CAUTION.

The smile and the softness left the woman as abruptly as they came. She once more was as brittle and thin as the limbs reaching in the fields. "It doesn't much matter what her name was. What's done is done." The widow stood, brushing at nothing on the front of her sweatshirt. Her hand rested on her stomach. "Seven dollars an hour and room and board is what I'm offering."

Julius leaned back, on his elbows, settling in to the stairs. He looked around, noting again the neglect. "You just bought this place?"

"My husband inherited it from his aunt. She never had any children, and he was the only son of her sister lost to cancer a few years back. My husband never knew his father. His aunt was all the family he had left, and it was her dying wish he have the farm. As soon as he heard the news, he hightailed it up from New Orleans, the handsomest man ever to set foot in Hope. Charming, too, with his Bourbon Street drawl and his sweet *'ma chère.'* He was all ready to unload the land and reap the rewards until he learned the property was zoned farmland and couldn't be sold to commercial developers. Kind of narrowed the field of prospective buyers to zero. He put the land up for sale anyway, and, in the meantime, married me for my family's money and influence.''

It was the way she recited the words without expression that let Julius know she'd been wounded.

''Two days after his death, I took the farm off the market.''

''You're a farmer, Mrs. O'Reilly?''

''Barely know the first thing about it.''

He chuckled. She just might be crazy.

''Until a short time ago, I never did anything except what was expected of me.''

He considered trying to make up his mind if she was nuts.

As if reading his thoughts, she said, ''They all think I went around the bend from the shock of my husband's death.'' She looked out to the gray, sturdy trees that had first drawn his eye. ''But this place is mine…my orchards, my fields, my land to dream on.''

He saw the same strength in her expression as he'd

seen in those thick-trunked trees and he understood. The woman wasn't crazy. She just wanted her own small square of the world where no one told you what to do or the right way to live your life. A place of your own. Home. He'd dreamed the same dream once, but in all his travels and in all this time, he'd never found it. Then he'd stopped looking. Just kept moving.

"There'll be a bonus though." Yes, she thought—a bonus, a perk. "At the year's end, after the first harvest, when the place is up and running—a percentage of the profits."

Julius looked around the run-down spread. "First, you have to produce profits. A percentage of nothing is nothing."

"There'll be profits, Mr. Holt." Such a strong, determined set to those narrow shoulders.

He pushed at his forehead, remembered his cap back on the seat of his truck and missed it once more. "You never farmed?"

"No." She didn't even try to hedge the truth. He again admired that. "But I'm reading everything I can get my hands on."

"Books?"

She straightened taller. "It's a beginning, Mr. Holt."

A beginning he thought, noting the house was built on a slight rise not too far from the road, giving a good view of the property all around. It was a pretty spot.

"So, you're a farmer, Mr. Holt?"

"Among other things," he said, appreciating the land's rise and fall.

"What other things would that be?"

"Let's see, I've been a sign painter, a laborer, an amusement park ride operator. I drove a truck up North, laid pipe in the South, worked the docks along the Mississippi." His crazy-quilt life spread out before him like the land circling him. "But mainly I've worked fields on both coasts and many in between. Apples and cherries in Washington, cotton and corn in Arkansas, peaches and peanuts in Georgia, potatoes in Maine."

"My, you do get around."

He eyed her, looking for mockery, but found none.

She ignored his sharp study. "Myself, I've never been much farther than the county line…except for school and summers when my father let the Aunties take me to the sea."

"You're kidding?"

"Do I look like a kidder, Mr. Holt?" Her smile this time was slim and self-deprecating.

"Never been no place? Why not?"

"Never had the desire, I suppose." She shrugged. "This is home."

The way she said it made something inside Julius twist inside out.

"Thank you for coming by, Mr. Holt."

He didn't rise from his relaxed pose on the steps. "A percentage of the profits after the first harvest? Is that all you're offering?"

She tipped her head up, a slight flare to her nostrils. "Exactly what do you mean, Mr. Holt?"

He looked around once more. "What about land?" The words surprised him.

She considered him. A broad, big-shouldered man who radiated power but moved with a surprising grace. His stare was too bold, his smile too easy, but his arms were strong and sturdy, and his wide, work-worn hands held a single blade of grass as delicately as if it were life itself.

"No offense, Mr. Holt, but you don't seem like a man who would still be here at the year's end."

The smile moved into his eyes now. "No offense taken, Mrs. O'Reilly. In fact, you're probably more right than wrong."

"Then why would you want land?"

He looked around once more—the ramshackle buildings, the peeling paint. "There's also a chance you could be wrong, Mrs. O'Reilly."

Lorna flattened her hand against her abdomen. Beneath the bulky sweatshirt, her stomach curved in. But it wouldn't be long before it swelled, stretched even beyond the loose fit of her sweatshirt. The ad had run five weeks. This was the first response she'd gotten. The men, even the untrained, unskilled ones, made more loading skids in her father's mill than she could pay. Maybe she was as crazy as they all said. She remembered the medal hanging around the man's neck, looked for it now. Saint Nicholas. Patron saint of travelers. Children. Old maids.

He touched the gold circle resting at the base of his throat. She stared at those fingers, that flesh, mesmerized, then snapped her gaze up. She should've been born a man.

"Do you want to see the workers' quarters?"

His mouth lazily curled. Every misgiving rose within Lorna once more. "Are you offering me the job, Mrs. O'Reilly?"

"I haven't decided yet." She was hard and straight and stern all over again. "Do you want it?"

His gaze wandered the land, then came back to wrap around her, that easy smile turning into a low roll of laughter. His blue eyes sparkled like temptation itself.

"I haven't decided yet, Mrs. O'Reilly."

Chapter Two

"What about land, Mrs. O'Reilly?"

She walked ahead of him, her steps smart as a soldier on dress parade. But her shadow stretched long and lean as pulled taffy. He watched the dark ramble of his own silhouette come up behind her.

"Land, Mr. Holt?" She didn't break stride nor turn her head.

"Land, Mrs. O'Reilly," he said to that stiff spine, its knobbiness visible even beneath the baggy sweatshirt. He'd bet her butt was clenched tighter than a miser's fist. He dropped his gaze, saw the twitch of round curves beneath the soft fabric and couldn't help but allow a man's natural admiration for a rear end riper than a California peach in mid-July. He forced his attention back up, let it rest on the jutting bone at the base of her long neck. He put a deliberate saunter into his words. "Seeing as you don't plan on paying much more than an insult and promising profits that might never exist, land seems to be the one and only sure thing you can afford to be generous with.''

Her clipped steps stopped. Several seconds passed before she turned. He could almost feel her clamping her teeth. He glanced at her clenched butt. God, she was fun.

She faced him, her nose raised and her gaze cooler than a January gale off the Canadian border. ''And what would you do with land, Mr. Holt?''

He bent down and plucked a piece of grass as if needing to always touch the ground around him. He didn't stick it in his mouth to chew on its new end as most would, but held it as before, between his thumb and forefinger, feeling its length. ''You can call me Julius, ma'am.''

She stared at those generous lips. His tongue, just the tip of it, flicked against their fullness, took a taste and then was gone. *No, I can't, Mr. Holt.* She waited silently for his answer, too aware of his size and strength and heavy, lazy sensuality.

He looked to the orchards leading to the lower fallow fields, the horizon uncluttered by the housing developments springing up outside the town quicker than goosegrass. His heavy gaze came back to her. His lips puckered and parted as if kissing the new spring air. ''I'd till it. Turn it until it was soft and moist and ready.'' He thought of the home he'd never found. He stared at the straight-backed woman, let his voice become thick with pleasure. ''Then I'd take off my clothes and roll across its width just to feel its sweet yield.'' He leaned in. ''Its sweet yield.''

A shiver moved up her spine, the sensation distressing in its pleasantness. She braced her shoulders, held herself even more erect. ''Like a hog, Mr. Holt?'' Her words were precise and pointed.

His full, finely shaped lips curved into a luring smile. His voice was languid. ''Like a man in love, Mrs. O'Reilly.''

Oh, those black gypsy curls. Those blue eyes where the devil lived. The wonder of that tender touch as his fingers met a common blade of grass. She remembered her late husband—and her vow never to be fooled again by false charm and faithless promises. Now a new moon had barely shone and already temptation had come in the form of Julius Holt. She studied the man before her, the muscled limbs, the powerful, dark sensuality of his face, the ease of his stance that spoke of a man secure in his ability to find and give pleasure. Physically he was twice the man as her deceased husband, and she didn't doubt twice the lover, for all her dead husband's pride in his prowess.

Oh yes, Julius Holt, with his leisurely smiles and comfortable sexuality, was the epitome of the type of man she'd vowed never to let get the best of her again—a rambling smooth-talker who made a woman go soft just meeting his smile. Could she have asked for a more perfect reminder of her own past foolishness? Her lips lifted in a tight curl. She could have laughed out loud. She'd never let him know it, but Julius Holt was exactly what she needed.

"I'll give you a stake of land, Mr. Holt—" she saw the surprise in his eyes "—if you're here at the harvest's end."

The surprise turned to amusement. "Is that a challenge, Mrs. O'Reilly?"

Her gaze was as steady as his. "I imagine it will be for you, Mr. Holt." Folding her hands at her waist, she spun and marched toward the barns. His low, pleased chuckle followed her. She tensed every muscle. He reached to pull the brim of his cap low in a satisfying tug and settled for another low roll of amusement, instead, as he took three strides and was beside the woman.

"Breakfast will be at five."

Damn, he hated farmers' hours.

"Lunch at noon. Dinner at five-fifteen." She kept her eyes straight ahead, her steps crisp.

"Not five-sixteen?" His tone was innocent. Her gaze cut to him. He gave her a wink. She snapped her head forward.

"You are to keep your quarters clean—including the bathroom."

"What time's inspection?"

She didn't even bother to look at him this time.

"You may use the washer and dryer on Sundays."

"Wouldn't it be easier if I just threw my skivvies in with your delicates?"

The woman halted, expressed a breath as she turned to him. "Do you hope to last here until the harvest's end, Mr. Holt?"

Hope. There it was again. The call that'd brought him here. He looked at the woman before him. Pure foolishness.

"This isn't going to work," Lorna decided before he answered. He was about to agree when a flash of soft defeat brought a humanness to her features.

Behind him, a woman's voice deep and hard as a man's called, "Lorna?"

Another voice, a high treble but equally adamant, blended with the first. "Lorna, dear?"

Lorna. Julius looked at the woman who'd fired him faster than she'd hired him. Her brow puckered as she expressed another long breath through her fine-cut nostrils. So that was her given name. *Lorna.* It fit her—the sound of it hard and soft like the woman herself.

"I told you she'd be here," the deeper voice flatly pronounced.

"Why, of course, she'd be here. Where else would she be on a glorious day like today but outside in the fine air?" the treble retorted.

"You said she'd probably gone to town."

"And you said she was in need of company. However—'' the light voice raised on a speculative note ''—it seems we were both wrong.''

Julius turned to see two elderly ladies crossing the grass. The smaller one wore a crocheted cape over a lace-collared dress and took dainty steps in low heels. The other woman wore a trench coat. Knit pants and flat loafers were revealed beneath the coat's hem.

''Aunt Eve. Aunt Birdy.'' Lorna welcomed the women. Julius heard the strain in her voice. ''What a surprise.''

The women drew near. The taller one in the trench coat with a helmet of steel-gray hair stared at Julius with open disapproval. ''I can't even imagine.''

The smaller woman, her features crinkling with good nature, stepped forward and extended her hand. ''How do you do, young man?''

He shook her hand. ''How do you do, ma'am.''

Tipping her head back, the woman took in the length of him, her eyes the same gray-green as Lorna's but sparkling. ''I'm so glad our Lorna is already receiving gentlemen callers. The early bird gets the worm, you know.'' Her smile went sly.

Julius gave her a wink.

''Aunt Birdy,'' Lorna protested.

''Don't be a ninny, Bernadette,'' the other woman said. ''Lorna's louse of a husband hasn't even been in the ground for a full season.''

The tiny woman smiled at Julius, holding his hand

in both of hers, but she spoke to the one Lorna called Aunt Eve. "It's been over a month, sister."

"A rat's ass. The date was—"

"Aunties." Lorna stepped forward, disentangling Birdy's hands from Julius. "Mr. Holt is no gentleman—"

"Indeed," Eve intoned.

"He's…" She glanced at him and straightened her shoulders. "He's my new foreman."

Julius looked at her with as much surprise as the aunts.

"He ran his family's farm in Oklahoma," Lorna continued, "and has also worked at establishments along both coasts as well as several in between. He has a wealth of experience."

Birdy beamed up at him. Eve glared. He smiled, gave her a wink, too.

"I was just showing Mr. Holt his quarters."

"Don't be ridiculous, Lorna," Eve snapped. "Your husband already threw away enough of your money—"

"God save his soul," Birdy interjected.

Eve snorted. "Too late for that. It's bad enough your husband squandered as much of your trust fund as possible. Now you're trying to finish the job by throwing the rest away on this sinking ship—"

"You should hear what they're saying in town, dear." Birdy's expression softened with sympathy. "It's quite upsetting."

"I know what they're saying in town. That I've gone off the deep end. 'Loony Lorna.' 'Lorna the Loon.'"

Birdy glanced at her sister, then back at her niece, the distress in her eyes confirming Lorna's claims. Julius saw Lorna's smile stiffen. Up until that moment, he might even have agreed with the town's assessment. But, until that moment, he'd never seen above that tense smile, pain so deep in those vulnerable gray-green eyes. Until that moment, he'd also never been a foreman before. *Foreman.* Even at seven an hour, he liked the sound of it.

"Actually, ladies," he said, "Mrs. O'Reilly's—"

"Lord, not that name." Eve turned to Lorna. "I thought you were going to go back to using the family name?"

Lorna said nothing. She was watching Julius, waiting to see what he was about to say.

"Mrs. O'Reilly's decision," Julius began again, "to run this farm was a wise investment."

Eve snorted. Birdy looked at Julius with her bright eyes. He squatted down to the new grass, pressed it to the ground. "Springs back up." He looked at the women. "Rich, moist, class-one soil. Fed first by the waters that left us that creek that splits the land, that pond in the lower field. Good irrigation sources. A little time, hard work and innovative planting…" He straightened to his remarkable height and released his killer smile. "In five years, our yields will be the envy of every other farmer around."

"Humph," Eve huffed. "The way farmers around here are trying to sell out to contractors, there won't be any left in five years."

"Then it's a good thing we'll be here. Now, if it's all right with you, Mrs. O'Reilly, and if you ladies will excuse me—" Julius tipped his absent cap "—I'll get started inspecting the equipment."

The women watched him as he headed to the buildings.

"I bet you could play tiddlywinks on that chassis," Birdy observed.

"Bernadette," Eve scolded as Lorna genuinely grinned for the first time in what seemed a long spell.

Eve turned to her niece. "Lorna, don't you pay no mind what the gossips say in town. The entire incident was more excitement than most of these chattering fools around here will see in a lifetime."

"I'm glad I've done the community a service then."

"Now, there's no need for a sharp tongue. And not everyone thinks you're off your trolley, but how can others even express their concern when you're hiding out here?"

"I'm not hiding out here."

"Of course you are," Eve insisted. "I don't care how many gaudy outfits you wear as if spitting at any offers of sympathy. And land almighty, child, what were you thinking with those shutters?''

''I don't want sympathy,'' Lorna said quietly.

Eve eyed her niece. ''‘The meek shall inherit the earth,' Lorna. And you should make an appointment with Doc Stevenson, have him check you for color blindness if we can get you back into town.''

''I have no intention of staying out of town. In fact, I'm driving in tomorrow for groceries and a few other things.''

''Thatta girl,'' Birdy urged. ''You walk down Main Street, head high, strutting your stuff. Who cares what they say? What happened wasn't your fault.''

Lorna's grin was long gone. ''Yes, it was, Aunt Birdy.''

''Nonsense. You were the victim in this entire debacle.''

Lorna cringed. ''I let myself be a victim.''

''Enough babbling.'' Eve waved her hand. ''The bottom line is this has gone far enough. It's time for you to come home.''

Lorna turned to her aunt. Past Eve rose the white house, once so plain and unadorned, but now distinct. Not far were the sturdy trees that would hang heavy with fruit at summer's end. She had land. She rested her hand on her abdomen. She had life.

And, now thanks to her impulsive announcement, she also had an employee—an irritating, provoking, wisecracking charmer who probably wouldn't stay any longer than to earn enough for a night of tall drinks and easy women. Yet, as of three minutes ago, she'd had someone on her side for the first time since she decided to live her life by her rules—not her family's.

She stretched her arms out as if to embrace all around her. "I am home, Aunties." For the first time, the words were real.

Eve threw up her hands. "Headstrong. Just like your father."

Lorna laid a hand on her aunt's arm. "Just like my father's sister."

Birdy agreed with an appreciative laugh. Eve scowled at both of them.

"Come." Lorna linked her arms through theirs. "Let me fix you a cup of tea and you can tell me what other news there is besides my mental instability."

Eve tsked with disapproval, but she watched her niece with worry.

Lorna squeezed her arm. "Don't fret, Aunt Eve. I'm fine."

"We can't help ourselves, Lorna. You're our little girl," Birdy appealed. "We're scared for you."

She pulled her other aunt close. "I'm scared too, Aunt Birdy. But for the first time in a long time, I feel…" Lorna tipped her head back, inhaled. "I feel like I'm breathing. Breathing deep."

Birdy looked at Lorna with bright eyes.

Aunt Eve snorted. "Foolishness. Farming. You're not a farmer."

"Truth is, Aunt Eve, I'm not sure who or what I am." Lorna held on tight to her aunts' arms. "Until about six months ago, I spent my whole life doing what one man said, hoping to please him. The next six months I spent trying to please another. And I never had an ounce of luck with either. You know why?" She stopped. Her aunts looked at each other, then warily at their niece. Lorna smiled, understanding even though no one else did. "I finally realized I can't please anyone else if I'm not pleased with myself."

"This?" Eve gestured impatiently. "This makes you happy?"

Lorna surveyed the land she was already in love with. She nodded, smiling. "Yes. This."

"Your father loves you, Lorna," Birdy put forth. "It's just that your mother…" Sadness dimmed her eyes.

"I know." Lorna squeezed her aunt's arm. "I know he loves me in his way, but I also know he's never gotten over losing his wife. And hard as I've tried, there's nothing I can seem to do to make it up to him."

"Well, for starters, you could've listened to him when he told you your late husband was after your money,'' Eve suggested. ''Would have saved us all a lot of trouble.''

''I know my marriage was a mistake.''

''Hell's bells, the whole county knows that.''

''But I don't regret it. It was that mistake that got me here.''

''Welcome to Paradise,'' Eve pronounced.

''Hush. Let the child be.'' Birdy's tone was so uncustomarily stern even Lorna looked at her with surprise.

Birdy smiled at her niece. ''Let's go have tea. I'll tell you all about the garden club's election. Myrtle Griffin declared it a coup.''

''Myrtle Griffin wouldn't know a coup if it jumped up and bit her in her girdled rear end,'' Eve declared.

''She called it a 'coup.''' Birdy stood her ground. ''And Pauline Van Horn said it was an abomination, an affront to the very principles on which the club was founded.''

''Oh no. Sounds like she's throwing her hat in the ring for town clerk again next year. If the woman spent less time posturing and more time tending her dahlias, she wouldn't have to blame the failure of her garden on everything from the European earwig to the ozone layer.''

''Dianthus,'' Birdy corrected. ''She has trouble each season with her dianthus.''

''Dahlias,'' Eve insisted.

Lorna smiled, the sound of the Aunties' incessant

quarrels as familiar and comforting as a mother's kiss.

It was heading toward the day's darkening hour when the aunts said their goodbyes, Eve adding admonishments and Birdy shiny eyed, looking at Lorna with silent entreaty. Lorna kissed them both, promising to see them soon, and hurried back to the house. She'd find her new employee after she figured out what she would do about supper. *Foreman.* What had possessed her? He'd want a raise now before he did a day's work. Well, he'd just have to be satisfied with the title.

She opened the yellowed refrigerator. Maybe if she cooked him a great meal, he'd forget about wages. But what could she cook him? She'd taken nothing out, not expecting to have to feed anyone except herself and her appetite tending toward the odd lately. She looked in the small freezer. There was a steak—not T-bone but not chuck either. She could add some fried onions, perhaps a potato or two if they hadn't gone and sprouted in the pantry closet bin. And there was that bread-making machine she'd bought on sale right after her elopement. Six weeks later she'd been a widow. Never even had time to get the machine out of the box.

She bent down to the bottom cupboard and found the bread maker behind the stacked bowls and glass casserole dishes. She slid it out, took it from the box and set it on the speckled counter. It was so white in this old kitchen. She stepped back. She should rough up those cupboards, paint them cantaloupe. She could already picture the faux wood doors gone, their dark surfaces replaced with an orange good enough to eat. She lay her palms soft to her stomach. Her late husband had been a cad, and she'd most definitely been an even bigger fool, so starved to hear the words ''I love you,'' she believed the first man who'd uttered them. Yet, as she'd told her aunts, her mistakes had brought her here. Now she just had to remember the lessons she'd learned, the vows she'd made. She moved back to the counter to start supper. One glance at Julius Holt with his cocksure grin and easy laughter in his eyes and she'd remember just fine.

THE BACK OF THE HOUSE SAGGED and wood showed bare where a piece of siding had ripped off and never been replaced. Julius stomped up the stairs, noting with disgust the second and third ones were loose. Enough work around this sorry place for ten men. But as he reached the back door, he smelled a bakery. Through the door's window, he saw Lorna standing at the stove, her stern gaze turned to the sound of his heavy steps. Still surprise flashed in her eyes, as if she hadn't expected him. He understood. He was just as surprised to find himself still here. With a queenly wave, she motioned him to come in.

He opened the door into a kitchen that smelled of

sweet heaven, the aroma of baking bread as thick as hay ready for cutting. He stood at the entrance on a brightly woven square of rug that he knew had to be Lorna's touch.

"Your company's gone?" He noted the linoleum was lifting in one corner.

She nodded and glanced at the clock over the refrigerator. "Supper's at five-fifteen. You're early." There was no surprise in her eyes this time. Only a scolding in her voice that made him smile. She turned her narrow back to his grin. She was a prickly one, all right. Man could hurt himself on all those sharp bones and hard lengths.

"So you meant it when you said I was the new foreman?"

"I always say what I mean, Mr. Holt," she told him without turning around.

"So that's the secret of your charm?"

She moved briskly from the stove to the sink, her profile unsmiling. "Might be a good time to bring your things into where you'll be staying. Did you see the trailer not far from the barns? It's open, been aired out. The water's turned on—"

"Hold up there. I don't remember exactly taking the job." His investigation had revealed the farm was in a sorrier state than he'd thought—broken equipment, a rusting tractor, roofs that looked like they leaked, apple boxes so old the pine was splintering away from the nails. It'd be backbreaking hard work getting this place up and running again with no help except for a woman with a hard spine and soft gray-green eyes who thought she could become a farmer by sitting in her front parlor reading.

Lorna turned on the water. "It was my impression we came to an agreement, Mr. Holt."

"It was my impression you hired me, then fired me faster than rabbits reproduce."

"Then I hired you again." Her voice was calm as a country morning, but she was scrubbing her hands too hard, too long.

"This place is in pretty sad shape."

She turned off the water, shook out a towel, swiped at the water splatters on the sink's edge. "Are you afraid of hard work, Mr. Holt?"

"No, ma'am. Work hard, play hard. That's my belief. Keeps life interesting." It also kept a person from thinking far into the night, remembering things better off buried.

She twisted the towel. "All right, seven thirty-five an hour."

"Ten dollars."

She wrung the towel. "Seven-fifty."

"Eight."

"Seventy seventy-five but not a cent more, and be sure you'll earn every penny of it."

"Plus the bonus at the season's end," he reminded.

She slapped the towel onto the counter. He smiled.

"Plus the bonus at the season's end. That's my final offer, Mr. Holt." She flung up the lid of a bulky-shaped, bright white appliance. "If you prefer to pursue opportunities elsewhere, that, of course, is your prerogative." She lifted out a loaf of perfect bread, brown, smooth crowned, the smell alone enough to make a man give thanks. She set it on a wire rack. "I wish you good luck and Godspeed."

That loaf of bread. His grandmother had made bread like that. And pies. Oh Lord, his grandma's pies. He could still see her, standing in a kitchen as old and dingy as this, her hard-knuckled hands cutting the lard into the flour, giving the bowl a quarter turn, cutting straight in again until the dough formed into soft crumbs. In late spring, there'd be rhubarb. Blueberry and peach would follow in the summer; apple and squash in the fall. His mother had been warned early in her marriage to stay out of her mother-in-law's kitchen, which suited her just fine since she had never been one much for cooking anyway. When they moved out West, whenever his father had mentioned pies, his mother had always declared she'd go to her grave without ever making a pie. She had, too. After his father had died, she'd pretty much stopped cooking altogether.

"Do you make pies?"

"This isn't a diner, Mr. Holt."

He smiled, the smell of the fresh bread sweet as a woman. He looked at Lorna, drawn up tight beneath her loose clothes. Even her high-and-mighty gaze couldn't take away the pleasure of that fresh bread. He breathed in deeply.

She paused a moment before turning back to the counter. "I'll get you clean sheets after supper…if you're staying."

Out the window the sun was making its way home. He smelled the bread, could feel those clean, fresh sheets. He would stay tonight. What he would do tomorrow, he'd decide, as always, when tomorrow came. "I'll stay." He turned to go.

"Did you mean what you said earlier?"

He looked at her over his shoulder.

"About the soil being rich, and our yields being the envy of other farmers? Or were you just saying that for the Aunties' benefit?"

Her expression stayed neutral, but beneath the careful tone of her voice, he heard the low leavening of hope. He remembered the hurt in her eyes earlier when she talked of the gossip about her. Yes, he'd said those things then for her aunts' benefit, but for her benefit also. Now he saw she needed to believe. And maybe, just maybe, he needed to believe a little, too. For both their benefits—hers and his—he said, "Seeds are no more than possibilities, Mrs. O'Reilly. Plant them, and anything is possible."

He opened the door. She cleared her throat. He glanced back once more.

"Thank you." The gratitude was so quiet and right in her voice, she turned away to the counter.

"You're welcome," he replied, his voice without overtones. He was still shaking his head when he reached his truck. A raise and a thank-you. Beneath that buttoned-up, tight-lipped exterior, the widow wasn't going soft around the edges on him, was she?

"Naw," he told the listening land. It'd take a lot more than an extra seventy-five cents an hour and a weak moment to prove the widow wasn't wound tighter than a fisherman's favorite reel. He gave a chuckle as he gathered his duffel bag. He left his sleeping bag stored in the narrow space behind the front seat. Tonight he'd have clean sheets, the thought alone bringing him enjoyment.

He started back across the yard. He couldn't say what tomorrow would bring, never could, but tonight he'd have a roof over his head, smooth sheets, a belly full of warm, fresh bread…and a promise of land. He looked at the fields' gentle curves, the trees waiting for new growth, the light coloring the sky. All was possibility.

No, he couldn't say what tomorrow would bring but, for tonight, he was here in Hope.

Chapter Three

Hell, he was late. He had gone to the trailer. Its rooms were narrow, and his head just missed the ceiling. But the bathroom boasted a stand-up shower with a Plexiglas door, and the bed on a bare metal frame was a double, not long enough for his length but big enough for his width. He'd dumped his bag next to the bed. A tall, plain dresser stood against one wall, but he didn't unpack. He never unpacked. He'd stretched out on the mattress, finding it surprisingly, pleasantly firm. He had closed his eyes, enjoying the support of the mattress, the ease of his muscles. He hadn't meant to take a nap. Now it was six thirty-five. He was an hour and twenty minutes late. Hell.

Still he forced himself to stop, catch his breath before he rounded the corner and reached the long length of yard where he could be seen from the house. He crossed the lawn, walking fast but not fast enough to show he was worried. He climbed the steps two at a time. Through the back-door window, he saw Lorna standing at the sink. She didn't look happy as she scrubbed an iron frying pan. He debated the wisdom of facing an angry woman with a weapon in her hand.

He chuckled low. He was the one going soft around the edges. He was late. That's all. It wasn't a felony.

He rapped on the glass, then opened the door without waiting for permission.

Her gaze shot to him, went back to the frying pan. "Dinner was at five-fifteen, Mr. Holt."

Whatever sliver of favor Lorna had found with him earlier was gone. "I had good intentions of—"

"The road to hell is paved with good intentions, Mr. Holt." She gripped the frying pan, scrubbing so hard her entire body twitched. He watched her scrubbing and twitching, her chin thrust out, her lips taut. He burst out laughing.

She spun around, soap bubbles and water spraying, and glared at him. "You find rudeness and complete disregard for rules amusing, Mr. Holt?"

Lord, she was more rigid than a cold corpse. Such control when she was about to split at the seams any second. Grinning, he stared at this ramrod of a woman. Was it the sheer challenge of her or the surprising glimpses of softness he'd witnessed earlier? Maybe it was her ironclad control that fascinated him—a man whose own lack of restraint had ruined his life…and taken another's. He wasn't certain, but he had to admit that this woman with her odd affections and strict routines and hints of humanness intrigued him as much as she chaffed at his well-developed good nature.

He let his smile go soft and lazy. "Call me Julius, darling."

Anger drained what little color she had. Her lips pressed into a hard white line. "Supper is over, Mr. Holt. Breakfast is at five."

He noticed the loaf of bread now wrapped in cellophane on the counter. When he looked back, he saw a thin triumph in those eyes gone the gray of thunderclouds. He would listen to his stomach rumble all night before he asked her for so much as a crust.

Then, as she was apt to do right when he thought he had her all figured out, she sighed and said, "Would you like a slice of bread, Mr. Holt?"

She was a puzzle all right. He glanced again at the bread. His stomach said yes but his pride said no. He didn't need Miss High-and-Mighty's charity.

He patted his flat stomach. "Actually I've been trying to cut back on my carbs."

Maybe it was the ridiculousness of his reply. Maybe it was the recognition of his pigheaded pride, as stubborn and strong as her own. Again Julius didn't know, but then, if he wouldn't be darned, Lorna's tightly pressed lips relented and a genuine,

amused laugh came from between them. His prediction had been right—Lorna O'Reilly's laughter did
sound pretty. He stared at her. This lady was a complete mystery.

She picked up the dishcloth again. "Kitchen's
closing, Mr. Holt. And I have some reading I'm anxious to get to."

"On how to be a farmer, Mrs. O'Reilly?" He
couldn't resist.

She rinsed the frying pan and set it carefully in
the drainer. She unplugged the sink, wrung out the
striped dishcloth and folded it neatly. Finally she
faced him, her hands clasped at her waist. "I intend
to make this farm a success, Mr. Holt. With or without you."

"Well, Mrs. O'Reilly—" he scratched his chest
as he stared at her "—the jury's still out on that
one." He turned and left.

As soon as the door closed, Lorna marched over
and locked it. She told herself not to watch him, but
she stood there even after his broad, tall figure disappeared around the corner. Inside her, she still heard
his rich laughter. Her hands tightened on the doorknob. She looked down to their betraying grasp.
They were raw knuckled, red and dry from the dish-
water. A spinster's hands, she thought. She had been
married, widowed, but her heart had turned cold in
the process. Now she had a spinster's hands...and a

spinster's soul. She pushed back the sadness that tried to creep in.

She knew Julius Holt, with his deep laughter and easy ways, saw only a dried-up shell of a woman. But she hadn't always been so self-controlled, so inflexible and rigid that she ground her teeth in her sleep. For a long time, she'd had no will at all and such a low sense of self, she'd done whatever her father deemed best. Then, for a brief time, she'd smiled all the time and walked with such a dance in her step, she'd barely felt her feet hit the ground. She'd been as foolish then as before, letting sweet lies and skilled kisses turn her silly though she'd known she was too tall and rawboned to be called pretty, too brash and efficient in manner to be alluring. Still she'd actually believed her handsome late husband had married her for love instead of the McDonough money. Her father had snorted she had acted just like a "woman." She'd been doubly humiliated when he'd been proved right.

The darkness was becoming heavier, blending shapes and shadows. But, in her mind, she still saw Julius with his heavy-lidded, dangerously blue eyes that seemed to look straight through to her soul—her spinster's soul—as if he too knew the longing and loneliness that lived there. The day hadn't even been done when the low roll of his laughter had caught her with a wash of warmness.

Already he made her feel something other than

wariness and fear and vigilant control. He made her feel what she'd vowed she'd never let another human being make her feel again. Vulnerable.

She closed her eyes, leaned her forehead to the cool glass. The hell of it was Julius Holt was perfect for her purpose. Not only was he a larger-than-life reminder of her past foolishness, but he also had the knowledge, the experience and the sheer brute strength she needed to succeed. She pressed her hand to her middle. She had to succeed.

She'd cut out her tongue before she'd admit it, but she needed Julius Holt.

Behind her closed eyes, she once more saw Julius's infuriating smile, those eyes like a starry night. And even as she gritted her teeth and fisted her hands, she heard the tiny prayer inside her. *Please stay.*

JULIUS WAS ON the back steps at four-thirty the next morning, smiling smugly as he enjoyed the gray ice sky of pale stars. He didn't know if it was his empty stomach or his need to show up the schoolmarm that'd led him here at this ungodly hour, but whatever it was, now that he was here, surrounded by the dawn's brittle dreamscape, he was glad.

He glanced at his watch. Four forty-five and still the house behind him was dark and silent. Wouldn't that be something if Mother Superior was late? He smiled, even though he knew it was an impossibility.

He was waiting for the sky's first streaks of blue, although the throbbing in his knee told him today's weather would be contrary, when he saw Lorna come out of the woods. She walked along the outer boundary of apple trees leading to the house. What'd she do? Stand sentry all night?

She was a bright spot as she moved through the morning, her coat opened, revealing a vivid orange T-shirt and high-perched breasts. The straight-legged denims she wore showcased a slim waist, nicely rounded hips and long, lean legs that scissored smoothly as she walked. She twisted her head side to side, then up toward the stars as if trying to work out a kink in her neck, and he saw her hair loose and soft in the vague light. She moved through the morning, determination and purpose in her every step and a solitariness about her that made him watch her and wonder. She was still some distance away and before she looked to the back porch and saw him, he watched her and thought her beautiful.

She spotted him. Her surprise was instantly replaced by vigilance, her stride checked by tension. Still she favored him with a closemouthed smile as she approached. "I see you'll not miss breakfast."

"I was beginning to worry it might be you who overslept this morning." He cocked an eyebrow. "Patrolling the grounds, warden?"

"Weather cooperating, I usually take a walk at this hour." She propped a sneakered foot on the bottom step and bent over to refasten a lace. "I find it clears the mind and quiets the heart."

A thousand teasing retorts were on the tip of his tongue as she raised her head. Their gazes met and for a breath, before she sharply turned, he saw in those still gray-green waters what he himself had known his whole life—faceless, nameless longing.

She straightened. He wasn't sure he hadn't imagined the moment in the dawn's crisp dream. Still he didn't speak. She mounted the stairs. "Last night you were late." She unlocked the door. "This morning you're early. Do you ever follow the rules, Mr. Holt?"

His soft laughter followed her up the stairs. "What do you think, Mrs. O'Reilly?"

She paused at the door, her back to him. "I think you wonder what good are rules if you can't break them?" She disappeared inside the house, his low, heated laughter following her. He sat smiling, enjoying the morning's beginning a minute more, when her lean shadow stretched across him. He turned to her long figure above him.

She cocked her hips, her hands on their pointy angles. "Are you planning on sitting out there all day?" She spun around before he could answer.

Julius chuckled. "Guess not," he said to the morning. He moved up the steps and into the kitchen to begin his day with Mrs. Lorna O'Reilly. His smile widened as he smelled the welcome call of coffee and the lingering traces of yesterday's bread.

"I started the coffee before I went for my walk." Lorna nodded in the direction of the coffee machine on the counter. "There are cups and spoons there. Creamer's in the refrigerator. Sugar's on the counter. I won't wait on you."

His eyes followed her as she moved about the kitchen, grabbing the skillet from the drainer, butter and eggs from the refrigerator. With aggravated breaths, she brushed at her hair as it fell from her shoulders and curved around her face, framing her sharp features. He poured a cup of coffee, leaned against the counter, and took a sip. "I like your hair down."

She cracked an egg against the skillet's rim. He waited for a stinging reply as she scowled down at the sputtering egg. But then her shoulders sagged. She glanced at him but didn't say anything.

He was almost disappointed. "Can I pour you a cup of coffee, Mrs. O'Reilly?"

"You don't have to wait on me either."

"It'd be my pleasure after all your warm hospitality."

She shot him a cool glance, but again said nothing. She reached and opened a drawer near the stove, fished out a rubber band and slammed the drawer shut. She flipped the eggs, moved the skillet off the burner, then marched into the hall. When she came back, her hair was secured into a low ponytail.

He chuckled and offered her the cup of coffee he'd poured. "Cream and sugar?"

Unsmiling, she shook her head as she took it from him and set it on the table, but as she moved back to the stove, she muttered, "Thank you." She slid the eggs onto a plate, angled the toast beside them and set the plate on the table. "I'll be going into town later to do some shopping. Tomorrow there'll be bacon or ham."

"Why, this is just fine," Julius assured her in his exaggerated way. She regarded him as if trying to determine whether he was sincere or sarcastic.

"Sit," she ordered, and turned back to the stove as if she'd reached a conclusion.

He sat down in the worn but clean kitchen smelling of coffee and baked bread on this clear, cool morning with sudden promise. He stared at the butter melting across the freshly toasted bread. It'd been a long time since anyone had cooked for him. He never stayed for breakfast. He looked up at the stern-faced woman. A few strands of hair had missed the rubber band and hung free and delicate along her elegant neck. "This is just fine," he said once more, softer.

She faced him, arched a brow. "You're not cutting back on proteins, too, are you, Mr. Holt?"

He grinned at her, then dug into his breakfast like a starving man. From the corner of his eye, he swore he saw a small smile on her face before she turned away.

"Aren't you going to join me?"

"I think not." She looked at the cup of coffee he'd poured her. Usually she had two to three cups, black, strong, relishing the bite of the bean. Now just the smell made her queasy.

He shoveled half an egg into his mouth. She felt her stomach roll. He waved his fork at her. "You'd better eat something or you'll be swooning in my arms once more."

"Excuse me." She bolted from the room. He chewed thoughtfully, then shrugged his shoulders and picked up another piece of toast.

He wiped traces of egg clean from the plate with the last triangle of toast, pushed the plate away, leaned back and sighed happily as he lifted his coffee cup. He'd had dreams as great as most men once, but he'd learned the luxury of a good meal and the freedom to get up and go when it was over was great happiness. Lorna still hadn't returned. He carried his dishes to the sink, considered them a second, then shrugged and washed and rinsed them. He grabbed the frying pan off the stove, filled it with soapy water but left it to soak. *Can't make her completely happy,* he thought, drying his hands on a paper towel. He considered pouring a second cup of coffee, but with his stomach full and the early morning contentment still flush upon him, he was anxious to get out to the land with its kind old roll. He looked to the doorway through which Lorna had fled, waited another second, then went to find her.

He walked down a hallway of scuffed bird's-eye maple to the first closed door. Beyond he heard labored breaths, then, with surprise, he recognized the liquid spill of retching.

"Mrs. O'Reilly?" He rapped on the door. "Are you all right?"

There was only silence, punctuated seconds later by another attack of illness. He winced, laid a hand to his own full stomach. He'd known such moments himself, but they were always preceded by a worthwhile night of hard drinking. He knew Lorna didn't at least have the satisfaction of a good night's drunk to take away some of the current situation's unpleasantness. He doubted Lorna had ever had a drink in her life, let alone gotten drunk. He doubted she'd danced much either or rolled in the hay for no reason other than she liked a man's look. He listened to her retching and couldn't help but feel bad.

The sounds subsided and were replaced by Lorna's stern voice. "Go away."

He stood undecided. He heard her heaving breaths. Poor Lorna. His sympathy came without thought. He didn't realize his fists had clenched until he felt his fingernails cut his palm. He forced his hands to uncurl. He hated to hear anyone in pain, he told himself. Still the image came—a man doubled over, blood pouring from his mouth, his nose, the taste of blood in Julius's own mouth. He closed his eyes. The image only came clearer. He heard Lorna's retching. He prayed for her, for him—no more pain.

When she opened the door minutes later, he was there. Her face, damp from the water she'd splashed on it, became even paler. She drew herself up.

He studied her. "Are you all right?"

She composed her features. "I appreciate your concern, but I'm fine, thank you."

He looked past her to the white toilet she'd just been leaning over. He looked back at her. "Come on then. Let's get you to a chair."

She stiffened as his hand wrapped around her elbow.

"Listen, you up and die on me, and I gotta go get another job." His hand stayed firm as he looked into those eyes that couldn't hide anything. Right now, he saw helplessness. Oh, she would be angry if she saw it.

"C'mon," he said gently.

She let him lead her to the table, pull out a chair, bring her a glass of water. She took a sip, set it down, staring at the room's corner. He saw her hands clenched in her lap beneath the table.

"Nothing to be uneasy about. I myself have spent many a night praying to the white porcelain god."

She shook her head, but her shoulders relaxed and,

with a surprising satisfaction, he listened to the soft, pretty sound of her laughter.

"You do have a way with words, Mr. Holt."

The color was coming back into her complexion. He leaned against the counter. "What? You never heard that phrase?"

Smiling, she shook her head.

"No? Aw, Lorna, where you been hiding from life all this time?"

Her smile dissolved. He realized his mistake.

"I mean Mrs. O'Reilly."

She looked to the room's far corner again. Her hands lay folded in her lap. "Well, it's not as if I'm especially fond of my married name." She looked at him, smiled a wan smile. "I suppose Lorna would do just as well."

Truth was she liked the way he said it with a hush of breath as if she were some rare, exquisite creature.

He raised his brows, stretched his features into an exaggeration of surprise that kept her smiling. "Does this mean you'll be calling me Julius?"

Most of her weakness was gone. "I imagine I'll be calling you many things before our association is through."

He threw back his head and released a loud laugh normally not heard at this hour of the morning. She felt the strength returning to her limbs. "But yes, I guess if you're going to stick around awhile—" she intoned it as a question but didn't wait for an answer "—we might as well be on a first-name basis."

"All right then." He nodded, looking strong and large in the little kitchen faded except for the throw rug by the door and her orange shirt. He pushed off from the counter and headed toward the door.

"I assume you know how to prune?"

"You assume correct." He reached the door.

"I've begun with the dwarf trees. You'll see where I've left off. I'll be out to join you as soon as I'm done in here."

He stopped and turned. "Storm's coming today. I need to get up on those roofs before it hits, see if it's all new shingles you need or if a patch job will do it. Repairs need to be done before the spring rains or—"

"Storm?" Her nostrils flared.

He nodded. "Snow."

She wouldn't even indulge him by glancing out the window. "Nonsense. There's been no prediction of a storm. It's going to be a beautiful day, warmer than yesterday. The roofs can wait. We'll start—"

"Storm's rolling in. My bum knee says so."

Lorna sat up straighter. "Your bum knee is not the boss here."

He leaned against the door. It was his slow cock-sure smile that did her in. She felt her stomach clench but knew it was too empty to threaten her now. Still it was a reminder of why she'd allowed this man to stay on—this man with the voice too warm and rich in the silent morning and the smile too quick and dizzying. She bit back her recommendation that if Julius and his omniscient knee couldn't do as told, they could move on.

"I've begun the dwarf trees," she fought him with a controlled, even voice.

He said nothing, leaning against the door, his pose insolent, his smile not wavering.

"The branches are newer, slender, most needing only a snip," she continued, assuming his compliance.

"I'll start with the old trees at the far south end."

She squared her shoulders. "*We'll* start where I left off, work our way back."

He stopped smiling. "Some of the old trees are so shaggy, I'll have to swing like a monkey to get to the top branches, and the heavier limbs need the saw. Once the storm comes it'll be too wet to climb and the damp bark will gum up the saw."

She stood. "We'll start with the dwarfs."

He crossed his arms across his wide chest, tilted his head, taking her in.

She met his gaze head-on. "You'll find the loppers in the barn."

He straightened. She girded herself for his challenge, but after a moment he only opened the door and left. To his credit, he didn't slam it, although she suspected that would have given him much satisfaction.

Through the door's window, she saw his broad, strong figure stride to the barn, his hands gesticulating as if he were talking to another. She had no doubt he was cursing her.

She thought of the way he'd said her first name only minutes ago. She shook off the memory as she moved away from the door.

Let him curse her. It was safer than listening to the hush of his voice when he said her name. First-name basis or not, she was still the boss. She couldn't let him forget that.

She looked out the window as she reached the sink. In the distant horizon the gray hadn't broken yet.

It was too early, she decided, turning her attention to the dishes. She saw the pan filled to soak, Julius's dishes washed and drying in the drainer. She'd never known any man—not her husband, certainly not her father—to even clear their plates from the table, let alone wash them. She picked up the dishcloth. What harm would it do if Julius checked the roofs before they started the pruning?

She shook her head. Give an inch now, and she'd never get it back.

"I'm the boss," she told the empty kitchen. She'd do well to remember it, too.

Chapter Four

Julius snipped a branch forking too close to its neighbor. He looked to the next and met Lorna's glance.

"Lovely day, isn't it?" Her breath clouded in the crisp morning air. He looked to the pale but sunny sky above, letting her have her moment of triumph. Then he looked to the far rise where the sky was filling in milky gray. Lorna turned to the horizon. Her expression soured. She turned back to the tree, refusing to look at him. He let a satisfied smile spread. She marched toward a slanting, unsuspecting limb, wielding her shears like a bayonet.

He moved to another branch and another, snipping, slicing, creating space, alternating the long-handled loppers with the saw for the particularly thick branches. The rich smell of wood and earth, so unlike the long colorless winter, surrounded him. There was peace here in the rows, in the *clip-clip* of the cuts, in the thought of a good bloom at the beginning of the growing season. He looked at the distant, larger trees, pruned by so many, they were as rambling as an old drunk. He should be climbing there, amid the wind damage and branches turning in on themselves. His sawing became unnecessarily swift. He slowed the motion of his arm. He'd be up in those trees soon enough. Not in the next day or two, but before the bloom.

Patience, he reminded himself. That was what the land taught. He looked to its lay, a piece of which had already been promised him. All farmwork took patience, perseverance. The land could give him that. And more. Roots. Peace. If he stayed.

He heard the fall of limbs in the next row where Lorna did battle. And if the widow didn't drive him crazy first.

At noon, Lorna ladled soup into a bowl and placed it beside grilled sandwiches. He ate lustily, washing the food down with great drafts of milk, his appetite made keen by the spring air and the awakening all around him. He didn't speak and neither did she. She kept her attention on the napkins, the salt-and-pepper shakers in the center of the table. He focused on his meal. From the corner of his eye, he saw her study go to him now and then. He waited for her disapproving frown of his coarse manners, but her expression became pleased, as if his base enjoyment of her simple fare also gave her pleasure.

She gathered her dishes and carried them to the

sink. "I'll be going into town after lunch." She broke the silence. "Is there anything you need?"

He was about to wipe his mouth with the back of his hand when she turned. He paused, her gaze steady on him. He reached for a napkin and patted his mouth daintily. Leaning back in his chair, he folded his hands across his full stomach. Before thinking, he released the belch that always bubbled up from a happy stomach. Now in her eyes, those easily read waters, he saw the disapproval.

"Mr. Holt—"

Uh-oh, he was a surname again. He supposed he should apologize. He didn't. Truth was, he liked the two bright pink spots in her pale cheeks. He wagged his finger. "Julius. Remember?"

"You'll do well to remember you're at the table, not a chicken coop."

He pretended indignation. "Now, that wouldn't be a slight on my late mother who raised chickens right in our front yard and loved them like they were her own babies."

She hesitated. "I didn't even know your mother."

"No, you didn't, so what right do you have to ridicule her attempt to provide for her family?"

"I didn't—I wasn't talking about your mother." Lorna's cheeks colored deeper. Julius's satisfaction expanded.

He broke out into a grin. "Oh, Lorna, you're too

easy. When are you going to learn not to take everything I say seriously?''

Her eyebrows raised. He mirrored the gesture. She stared coolly at him. "Actually it should be hard to forget that yours isn't a serious nature."

He stretched out his legs and settled himself more comfortably in the chair. "Laugh, Lorna. It'll keep the blood flowing."

She stood stiff as starch before him. "I laugh plenty."

He raised his eyebrows again. She shifted self-consciously.

"Just not lately."

He nodded. "Fair enough." He too had known times when laughter wouldn't come. Until he realized if he didn't laugh, all he'd have left was pain. So, he'd taught himself to smile like a man without a care, move on like a man without a hope of home, staying always one step ahead of the past. He silently asked the tall, straight-backed woman, was that what she had done? Leaving her father's wealthy house, moving to the edge of Hope to this ramshackle farm? Was she, like him, only trying to stay one step ahead of the pain? He would teach her to laugh then.

"I'll go with you into town."

"I don't think so."

He grinned, always amused by her. "I need to find out where I can get tractor parts."

"Field's Equipment." Lorna went to the sink and turned on the water.

He roused himself from the chair and piled his own dishes. "That's where I'll go then. There's a beaut of an old Massey Ferguson, but it might be tough finding the parts for it. And the John Deere should have new plugs, belts—"

"The trees need pruning." Lorna rinsed a plate and placed it in the drainer.

"And the tractor needs fixing."

He was beside her, big even against her long spare frame. She rinsed off a bowl, ignoring him. "Make a list of what you need, and I'll pick the things up for you." she told him. She paused as a ripple of nausea took her stomach. She waited for another, but none came. Some days the sickness was only mornings; some days not.

"I'll take care of getting the parts."

Now she turned to him. He stood so close, she saw the shadow of new growth across his jaw. She looked away. "I'm perfectly capable."

"Better if I deal with it."

Her gaze snapped back to him. "Why?"

He leaned in. She smelled the outside, sensed a raw strength. She wanted to step back. She'd be damned if she did.

"Trac-tor parts," he said slowly, as if speaking to a child.

"I understand English."

He leaned in farther as if to tell her a secret. "It's a man's area."

She repressed an urge to stamp her foot. She settled for tipping her head back and eyeballing him in all his Neanderthal glory. "This is the twenty-first century, and granted, while Hope isn't exactly a cosmopolitan area, we are—"

"You always do that?"

His question stopped her. "Do what?"

"Talk like your underwear is wedged up your butt?"

"Mr. Holt—"

"Uh-oh." Julius rolled his eyes. "Here it comes."

Her teeth clenched so hard he feared lockjaw. The fire in her eyes heightened, favoring the green over the gray, and the two bright pink spots of color that made her seem sassy and alive returned.

"Your extraordinary insolence—" She heard herself. She stared out the window, the color in her cheeks and the fire still in her eyes.

He studied the strong proud line of her profile—a woman who wouldn't turn doughy and lax as the years came but would remain fiercely handsome.

She faced him, her eyes resigned. "Panties up the butt talk?"

He gave her low laughter. "Major wedgie."

She sagged slightly against the sink. To his surprise and, he suspected, her own, she smiled. A second later, the smile turned into light laughter, making her face pure pretty now and the kitchen warm as home. He listened, her laughter falling on him like a new wind.

She was bright-eyed and her voice held a rare flirty softness as she asked, "I'm learning, aren't I? To laugh?"

Lord, if he couldn't aggravate her, he just might have to fall in love with her. He stepped away.

She pulled herself up as if also realizing the sudden drop of defenses. Her features returned to their set, strong mask. She walked to the table, swiped it clean, catching the crumbs in the flat of her hand.

He waited as she walked to the sink and brushed the crumbs into the garbage. He was about to continue the argument when, as always, surprising him, she said, "I'll be leaving in twenty minutes. Be ready if you're going."

Exactly twenty minutes later Lorna marched out of the house. She wore a beige jacket. The temperature had risen, as it always does before a storm, but she'd wound a thick tomato-red scarf round her neck anyway. She strode in gaily striped sneakers to her sensible compact. She opened the driver's door and looked at Julius who was standing nearby, watching her with an amused expression.

"Are you coming or not?"

"In that sardine can?" Julius let his laughter roll to her. "Where do you want me to ride—on the roof?"

She looked at him blandly. "Suit yourself." She disappeared inside the car.

He walked to his pickup. As he reached the driver's side, he looked at Lorna's car idling in the driveway. She was gazing straight ahead, her jaw in its familiar firm set. He opened the truck's door. He should jump in and drive fast to the county line and keep going until this humorless woman and her run-down farm were far behind him. Yet he stood there, staring at her frozen profile, that scarf the red of a matador's cape as if chosen to deliberately provoke. Damn the scarf. And damn the woman, he cursed as he slammed the door and headed toward the car and that bright streak wound about that long, stiff neck. He'd almost reached the car when it rolled into reverse and came slowly down the driveway heading straight for him. He stepped to the side. Lorna swung her head to check behind her. She blinked in surprise when she saw him. Still she pursed her lips and continued to ease the car out of the driveway. He tapped on the driver's window as it drew alongside him. She braked, pressing down too hard. Her slight body lurched into the steering wheel. She yanked herself up, rolled down the window and looked at him with arched brows and those sculpted nostrils breathing harder than usual.

He tipped his head toward the truck. "I'll let you drive."

Her glare went away from his smile to his truck.

He glanced back at the vehicle with the rust spreading up from its undercarriage but, otherwise, the most solid and dependable relationship Julius had ever had.

"All right." He exaggerated his sigh of surrender. "You can pick the radio station, too, but I've got to warn you—if any opera comes on, I'm singing along."

The muscle in her jaw twitched as if she either wanted to smile or scream. Instead, she snapped off the car's engine and swung open the door, barely missing him as he jumped back. Without a word, she walked to the pickup, climbed up into the cab like a queen ascending a throne and sat stiffly, gazing straight ahead at nothing particular.

They rode in silence, Lorna watching the landscape she'd known since her first breath, and Julius wondering what that was like and whether his silent passenger deserved sympathy or envy? He smiled, knowing Lorna wouldn't accept either—not from him. Not from anyone.

The land became more populated. New vinyl-sided capes and half-bricked low ranches sat squarely in the center of fresh-seeded lots, a single tree in each yard, planted equal distance from the house and the road. As they neared the town's center, Lorna's hands worked in her lap, picking and gathering at the heavy cotton of her coat.

Julius knew if he asked, "Nervous?" she'd deny

it with an irritated, ''Don't be ridiculous.'' Still he remembered her face when she'd said the names given her by the townspeople. ''Loony Lorna.'' ''Lorna the Loon.'' He watched her tangling fingers and found himself searching for a way to put her at ease. He knew what it was like to be the object of whispers and averted glances or plum unrepentant open stares.

''I can drop you off at the grocery store and run my errands and come back for you. Or would you like me to wait for you in the parking lot while you shop?''

Her wary expression questioned his polite tone. ''That doesn't seem very sensible, does it?''

''No, ma'am.'' From the corner of his eye, he could see her assessing, trying to decide if she'd detected sarcasm in his tone or not.

''Drop me off at the door and come back for me after you've finished your errands. I won't need over an hour and a half though, so don't make me wait.''

''No, ma'am.'' He saw her sharp look but her hands had been still in her lap for the past several seconds.

They came to a crumbling brick cotton mill, undoubtedly once a primary source of employment, but now only a sign that they'd reached the main part of town. On a hill opposite the brick building rose a sprawling white-columned beast of a house looking down on Hope. Still trying to occupy Lorna, Julius gave a low whistle. "Who lives there?" he asked, curious but mainly seeking to stay Lorna's tangling fingers. "The mayor? The madam?"

Lorna didn't even look up at the white house hovering over the town. "My father."

He glanced at her. She ignored him. He looked back at the house that spoke of wealth and power. "That's where you grew up? In that house?"

"It is my father's house. I have my own house now."

"And your freedom?"

"Yes," she said firmly.

He understood. Power and wealth and his own weakness of will had imprisoned him once, too.

They drove through the main street, past the storefronts tight as a strip mall, to the large supermarket at the end. Lorna's hands began to twist once more in her lap, but he couldn't help her now, his thoughts unexpectedly caught in a past he didn't want to remember.

"The grocery store is up on the left." Lorna unsnapped her purse and searched until she found her grocery list. She scanned it. "You don't have any food allergies, do you?"

He heard this so-Lorna-like question. A grin slowly crept onto his face.

"I didn't think so." She snapped her bag closed, held it upright on her lap.

He looked at her, this daughter of riches and power, with her garish sneakers and sensible questions, her colorless face contrasting even paler with the strangling red scarf, and he was strangely soothed.

"I'm not particularly partial to sushi...unless of course, it's cooked right." *Laugh, Lorna.*

"First of all, sushi is mainly served raw and secondly, the SuperSave wouldn't carry..." She stopped, seeing the easy smile on his face, telling her to laugh at him...and herself. But she couldn't. Not now. The truck turned into the supermarket's parking lot. She stiffened, said nothing more as her hands clenched the large pocketbook square in her lap.

Julius stopped the truck alongside the store's entrance.

"I'll not be much more than an hour, an hour and a half at the most. You'll not make me wait?" It was a question now, instead of a command, and he knew her nervousness had taken hold.

"Smile, Lorna," he said with that unexpected gentleness that fascinated her.

She opened the truck door and climbed down. "Don't make me wait."

He winked at her. "No sushi. Unless you can cook it right."

She exhaled a long breath as she shut the door. He waited as she walked to the entrance, her steps even, her shoulders high. As the automatic door swung open, she turned to the idling truck and mugged a smile. He smiled back, put the truck into gear. She'd be all right.

She turned around, tempering her smile but keeping it firmly on her face as she pushed the cart toward the produce aisle.

JULIUS DELIBERATELY SMILED, TOO, as he entered Field's Equipment Sales and Service. Move with the wind, care little for anything and smile, always smile, as if a good time were around every corner. It was far from salvation, but still it was something.

He took his cap, stuck it in his back pocket. "Afternoon, fellas."

The heavyset man behind the counter nodded, watching Julius approach. A thin man in stained coveralls sitting on a metal chair behind the counter stared, unsmiling. Julius long ago had grown used to the wary looks. He'd always been the stranger in town.

"Any chance of getting a water pump for a '75 Massey Ferguson 130? I'll need a tune-up kit for a 420 John Deere, too."

"The tune-up kit we've got in stock, but a pump for an MF 130…" The man at the counter whistled low as he pulled out a thick catalogue. "That might take some time to find." He rifled through the pages. "George" was embroidered in red thread above his front shirt pocket. "Don't believe we've done business before. Own a farm around here?"

"Just working one for a while."

"That a fact?"

"Pretty little spread east of town."

George glanced over at his colleague in the corner, then back at Julius, assessing him.

"Managing the place for a Mrs. Lorna O'Reilly," Julius supplied. "Nice lady who's had a rough time of it recently, losing her husband and all."

He moved to a rack of filters near the counter, removed one and turned it over to read the back of the package. "That must've been really something."

"Made the Boston papers." The thin man joined the conversation. "They say she ain't been right since."

Julius heard the fishing in the comment. He took another filter off the rack, turned it over, feigned interest. "She seems all right to me."

The thin man snorted. "You wouldn't have thought so if you'd seen her at the funeral, all done up in this dress so green and bright it hurt your eyes to look at it."

"Well now, I'm new to these parts so I could be mistaken, but I don't think it's a law a person has to wear black to a funeral."

"It's disrespectful," George said.

"Downright blasphemy," the thin man added.

Julius set the filter on the counter. He had promised himself he'd walk away before ever putting his hands on another man again. Yet here he was courting trouble, purposely provoking these men. For what reason? The hostility in the men's faces told him it was time to say no more. Then he remembered Lorna's brave smile as she'd stepped into the grocery store.

"Kinda like sleeping with another man's wife?"

The thin man's expression didn't become any friendlier. "The only thing about that affair was its surprise ending. Heck, everybody knew Lorna's husband married her for her daddy's money. And nobody knew it more than 'the Boss.'"

"'The Boss'?"

"Lorna's old man," George said. "Axel McDonough, but everyone calls him 'the Boss,' account of he owns most of Hope."

"And is hated about as much." The thin man spit into a paper cup. "Especially by his late son-in-law."

"The feeling was mutual," George pointed out. "'The Boss' had the guy pegged as soon as he came a'courting. Now, if the poor fool had been from around here, he would have known better. And he wasn't really a bad guy, either. Everybody liked him."

"Obviously not everyone," Julius smiled friendly-like at George.

"Well, the ladies all liked him, I can tell you that."

The thin man grinned. "And he liked them right back."

"Seemed to have a fondness for the married ones," Julius noted.

George shrugged. "He said it kept things less complicated that way."

Julius kept an amiable smile as he said, "Guess he was wrong."

The thin man eyed Julius. "Wasn't his first mistake. Only his last. 'The Boss' told him to stay away from Lorna, that he'd never see a dime of the family's money. Some say he married her just for spite."

"Didn't hurt Lorna had some resources of her own," George added. "Might have even been the end of it, too, if he hadn't started sleeping around—"

"Shoot, he'd never stopped," the other man interjected.

"Maybe not, but now it was Lorna's money— *McDonough money*—he was spending as fast as he could on these other women and anything else that struck his fancy." George looked Julius square in the eyes. "No one makes a fool of 'the Boss.'"

Unlike his daughter, who wasn't so lucky. Julius thought again of Lorna's shaky smile and solid step as she'd walked into the grocery store. "What happened to the man who shot Lorna's husband?"

"Lawyer pleaded temporary insanity. Got a stint

in the state hospital for seven years, probably be out on good behavior in three.''

''What about his wife?''

''She moved back with her mother two counties over. Heard she visits him every other weekend.''

''Some story, huh?'' The wiry man grinned at Julius.

Julius thought of Lorna, her dictator of a father, her loveless marriage, an ordinary man driven to murder another. ''Some story.''

HE WAS LEANING against the truck in the grocery store's parking lot when Lorna came out, pushing a cart stacked high with bags. As he started toward her, a big-haired woman stopped her. The woman lay a comforting hand on Lorna's forearm, but he saw the keen curiosity in her face. Lorna's features were strained. He walked a little faster.

''Let me take these for you, Miss Lorna.'' He smiled at the other woman, touched the bill of his cap as he wheeled the cart out from beneath Lorna's death grip.

Lorna looked at him, surprise and a streak of relief coloring her expression before she schooled it neutral. ''Sylvia, this is Julius Holt. He's managing the farm for me.''

He liked the way she always said it like that— ''managing the farm''—not working, not just hired but "managing," expressed in that schooled, cultivated tone—as if he really were somebody.

Sylvia regarded him. The surprise stayed in her eyes. "Hello." The curiosity increased. "You're not from around here, are you, Mr. Holt?"

"Can't say I'm really from around anywhere, ma'am. I began in the West and just seemed to have blown East." He smiled the smile he knew women always returned. Sylvia with her big hair and big, interested eyes was no exception.

"A tumbleweed then, Mr. Holt?"

"That's me, ma'am. I blow where the wind takes me but this time I was fortunate enough for God's sweet breeze to bring me to Miss Lorna's place."

"Is that so? Why, you sound like a happy man, Mr. Holt."

"Ma'am, you must know about her place? Sweetest soil this side of the Mississippi."

"Really?"

"Now Julius," Lorna demurred, "I'm sure Sylvia has better things to do that stand around the supermarket talking about dirt."

"Dirt? Dirt? It's the food of life, rich as the world itself. You must come out and see it for yourself, ma'am. I'm sure Miss Lorna would love to have you visit and it'd be my personal pleasure to show you around."

"Maybe I'll do that, Mr. Holt," the woman said with a silvery promise in her tone.

"Julius, ma'am."

"Julius." Sylvia held his gaze a moment longer, then turned to Lorna. "I'm so glad everything is going well after…well, you know. You seem to be doing okay. I was a ninny to worry, wasn't I?"

Lorna stopped staring at Julius only long enough to address Sylvia. "I'm doing fine."

Julius smiled at them both. "We'll be expecting you soon now, Sylvia."

She smiled. "Soon."

"You laid it on a little thick, didn't you?" Lorna asked as soon as they were out of hearing distance.

"What?" Julius pretended innocence.

"'Miss Lorna,'" she mimicked in his baritone. "What was that all about?"

"Just showing some respect. Maybe back home it's fine to be on a first-name basis with you, but in public, it's only proper I address you with due respect. You don't want people to talk now, do you?"

"It'll take more than a 'Miss Lorna' to quiet them." She shook her head and repeated, "'Miss Lorna.'"

"Now you said yourself you're not too fond of your present last name, so 'Miss Lorna' it was."

Her lips twitched, the smile that'd been pressing almost evident. "Well, the smooth talk was suddenly thicker around here than black flies after the thaw. I wouldn't be surprised if Sylvia didn't come traipsing out to the farm, lured by charm as much as curiosity.''

He loaded the grocery bags into the truck bed. ''You should have visitors. You should throw a pig roast and invite the whole town.'' His dark blue eyes met hers. ''You've got nothing to be ashamed about.''

Lorna snatched the empty cart to wheel it back to the carousel. ''I'm not ashamed.''

''Darn right you're not,'' Julius's declaration followed her.

She came back and climbed up into the cab. He put the truck into reverse and they headed for home.

''Myself, I think you're a brave woman.''

''Brave?'' She laughed dryly. ''I may not be crazy like they say but no, Julius, I'm not brave either.''

''Sure you are. Why, you could be living high on the hog right now in that white house on the hill.''

Lorna shook her head.

''Yet here you are—taking over that farm, starting over.''

She kept shaking her head. ''If I had real courage, I wouldn't even be here in Hope. I'd run as far as I could.''

''Don't take any courage to run. Running's easy,'' he said, his eyes on the highway.''But you picked yourself up by your bootstraps and made a new life. Most would still be sitting around, licking their wounds.''

She looked at his strong features contrasting with his long, dark curls. She suddenly wanted to say quietly, so quietly, *I'm scared to death, Julius. Downright terrified.* She folded her hands in her lap and turned her gaze to the road.

They drove in silence the rest of the way until they were almost home. Julius smiled and pointed past the windshield. "Look."

Lorna followed the direction of his finger. It had begun to snow.

Chapter Five

Julius raked the edges of the fire, burning the brush from the last of the pruning. It'd taken several weeks of steady work to finish all the trees, but, working together with a woman as determined as he, the job was finally done. The snow he'd predicted had lasted only two days before the sun turned strong and melted it. Still, for the remainder of that first week, the branches had been too wet to climb, too soft to saw…and Julius had strutted as he'd gone about the many other tasks, Lorna always at his side. During the day, she followed him like a shadow as he worked, asking him too many questions, until he sighed and rubbed the base of his skull as though a headache had lodged there. But he showed her how to spread fertilizer, hang insect traps, grease an axle, note the pond moving from glassy white to gray mush. It was the season of preparation, never-ending repairs, small jobs, plans, measurements, always with an eye on the sky and the talk of May blizzards that had destroyed entire apple crops years past.

Julius lifted his eyes from the smoldering fire. From where he stood, at the orchard's far rise, he could see almost the whole farm. He leaned on his rake, his gaze scanning the lower pastures. *Raspberries,* he'd told Lorna, nodding to the right square. *Blueberries,* he said, indicating the opposite stretch, talking as if his future was no farther than those pale, softening fields. He looked past the land to the bordering woods where the hemlocks were preparing their yellow-green buds.

So many landscapes over the years, none seen twice.

He turned his attention back to the brush, his thoughts to the work, of which there was enough to occupy ten men's restless minds. He had to finish spreading the fertilizer; the grass would need mowing; more of the brush would be mulched and spread at the base of the trees to form a clean circle.

The fire was dying to ash. He reached down to the ground, let the soil sift through his fingers. He smiled. He hadn't been lying to Lorna when he'd said the land was good, fed by the rivers all those years ago. It was dark, rich, no clay pan. Good land. A piece of it had been promised to him. He straightened and checked the fire a final time, then turned to more brush piled high, readied for mulching. He adjusted his cap and had started toward it when an object in the grass caught his eye. He stopped and studied the spot, saw a movement. He headed toward it.

LORNA OPENED the oven door to check the meat loaf. She straightened, lifted the cover of a pot bubbling on the stove and stuck a fork into the center of a potato chunk. When it split apart, she turned off the burner and carried the pot to the sink to drain it. The steam rose, flushing her face, dampening the stray hairs that had loosened while she'd worked in the orchard. She looked past the seedlings on the windowsill that Julius had taught her to plant. The sun was still warm, and what had first been all mud was being dried by a keen wind and hotter days.

She was setting the milk on the table when Julius came in, his hands cupped to his chest, covering his heart.

"Look."

He came close to her. She smelled spring and hard work. He opened his hands as if offering her a treasure and, in his palm, warmed by his chest, soothed by the beat of his heart, slept a newborn rabbit.

"I almost stepped on the little fella, he's so small. He must be the runt."

She touched the new soft crown with the lightest of fingertips.

"I searched for his nest, but the fires must have frightened his family, and they moved on. Poor little guy. He probably couldn't keep up and got left behind. He's so small, I almost stepped on him," he repeated.

Lorna glanced up. His face was grave.

"You hold him, here." He gave her the tiny creature without waiting for her permission. "Cup your hands like so and put him to your heart. He likes that. I'll go get a box from the barn, line it with a flannel shirt."

"I have a shoe box upstairs and an old sweater, if you want to use it," Lorna offered. "You could put the box near the stove. He might like that, the warmth."

Julius nodded and took the bunny from her so she could gather the things to make his bed. After the baby was cozy in the cushioning folds of her sweater, they ate. When they finished, Julius took his dishes to the sink and squatted down beside the box.

"Is he okay?" Lorna stepped beside Julius on her way to the sink.

"He's okay," Julius said softly. He offered his hand. The baby licked his fingertips. "They like the salt," he told her.

Lorna observed the man, the longish tumble of dark curls, his size terrifying, his broad hand offered tenderly to the tiny creature. She didn't know this man at all, she realized. Not at all.

THE NEXT MORNING, not long before dawn, after she'd put the coffee on, she lifted the soft ball of bunny and kissed its sweet crown. Warming it against her chest, she stood at the east window as she did each morning. She told herself it was because here the day's first warmth entered. But she knew she was seeking more than the sun. She was watching for Julius. Now that he was here and she'd begun to believe the farm would succeed, she couldn't help but ask how long he would stay. She didn't think the mere promise of profits or land could hold a man like that. She wasn't sure anything could hold a man like that. He looked at the land as if it were Eden itself, but then those blue eyes went to the blue of horizon, and he stared too long, and she knew he was thinking, *Away, away.* She had let her ad in the Help Wanted section continue to run. And every dawn, she stood here, watching, wondering if today was the day he wouldn't cross the yard with his curiously swift yet soft movements.

Be a blessing, she told herself. It was only the increasing light each day, the coloring of the short, dead grass on the house's south side, the knowledge of a mystery taking place within her womb right now that had allowed her so far to tolerate his efforts to aggravate her. That and the fact she needed his raw strength and innate knowledge. She dismissed the thought, as soon as it rose, that she actually enjoyed the give and take, the needling. She'd never taken well to teasing, always too acutely aware of her shortcomings and the truth beneath the taunts. Yet this sparring with Julius was different from painful remembrances. On the surface, yes, it seemed as if they were at odds, but underneath, an awkward connection was being created.

Lorna felt for any slight roundness to her stomach but it still pressed flat against the counter's edge as she stood, waiting for the dawn to come. Fortunately, she was so tall and wide-hipped, it would take longer for the physical changes to show on her, the doctor had told her at her first visit. He'd then pronounced her too thin—she'd actually dropped a few pounds the first months—but otherwise she was fine. The morning sickness had pretty much passed. Only now and again, her stomach would roll and she'd have to hurry, hoping to get the bathroom door closed and the water running in the sink so Julius couldn't hear. Not that she was hiding the pregnancy, although it wasn't anyone's business but her own. The subject just hadn't come up yet. In the meantime, she didn't like anyone—most of all Julius—to see her like that—sick, weak, bent over...what did Julius call it? The white porcelain god. She smiled to herself as she stood at the window. Outside the darkness was easing. In the midst of the vague light, Julius came. The day had begun.

JULIUS STOOD up from the apple crates he'd been inspecting, almost knocking over Lorna. "Lord, Lorna, let a man breathe."

She didn't even glance up from the small notebook she always carried and was busy now jotting down facts in her small, precise handwriting. Her pink tongue darted out, wet the tip of her pencil as she turned the page and continued. Pages of notes preceded that one. Even after a full day in the fields, Julius had seen her light on late at night and known she was reading the texts she'd gotten from the Co-operative Extension.

"I may be a stubborn woman, Julius, but I'm not stupid. I need your knowledge." She continued to write.

"Well, I need to go about my work without tripping over you every five seconds." In reality, the way the woman listened to him with her head tipped, her features intent and her pencil flying across the page pleased him. He would explain something he seemed to have been born knowing, and she would receive his words with such a wonder and gratefulness revealed only by those truth-speaking eyes, he would have to turn away. And in the barn's dusky warmth, for the first time in so long, he would feel no need to leave. It was then he couldn't resist riling her.

"What would you have done if I'd never showed up?"

"I don't have the time nor the inclination to deal in 'what ifs.' You're here. That's what matters."

He watched her hands dancing across the lined

paper, the barn's shadow light turning her hair a color richer than the earth, her features still and serene.

"You're a librarian, not a farmer."

"For now," she answered as she scribbled into her notebook, so excited she forgot to be irritated. She finally finished, looked up at him with bright eyes. "Only for now."

He shook his head, but she saw his taunting smile gentle as if something about her strange ways pleased him. She took a step back, concentrating on her notebook until the words became clear again.

He started out of the building. "Well, try not to crowd me in the meantime."

She followed right behind him. "To think, I could be off with the Aunties right now, shopping and enjoying myself instead of standing here, listening to your grumbling."

He stopped so abruptly in the doorway, she collided into him. She jumped back from the muscle and hard strength and warm skin. He glowered down at her.

She tipped her head to meet his glare. "I should have said, 'Yes, I'll be there with bells on,' when the Aunties called this morning and invited me to a most pleasant afternoon of lunch and shopping."

"So why didn't you?"

"Excuse me." She paused for effect. "But there's

a little too much to be done around here.'' She tried to move out the doorway.

''Yeah, well, I certainly could've used the peace and quiet for a change.''

She swiveled her head toward him. He waited for her retort in her clever, flat tone. She angled her chin an inch higher, but, without even one dry word, she pushed past him and marched across the yard to the house, her rear end twitching back and forth so that he had to watch, fascinated, and concede she still had the upper hand. Not long after, he heard the back door slam and looked over from the apple trees to see her marching to her car. He stood in the sun, smiling as she drove off, this woman who confounded him as much as made him grin, and thought, *I should be moving on.*

He took off his cap to wipe his brow, seeing the sun directly overhead. He crossed the yard and went into the house. As the sun grew stronger, the kitchen smelled of past seasons—apples and root vegetables and wood smoke. She had given him a key for when she was out, but only the front door was locked anymore and that was only because the back entrance was the one they used.

He looked in the refrigerator before washing up in the laundry room's deep-tubbed sink. With satisfaction, he saw the platter of cold chicken left from last night's meal. He shut the door and started toward the washroom when he heard the sound of a car coming down the road, pulling into the driveway, stopping. A car door slammed.

"Should have known the guilt would get her before she even got to the main road," he said as he walked to the laundry room. "There goes my peace and quiet." But he knew the words were said aloud even now to break the silence. Truth was he'd gotten used to the routine of sharing his meals with someone. Truth was he'd gotten used to sharing his meals with Lorna. He should be moving on, he thought again.

He stopped in the hall as the front doorknob twisted. "Must have missed me more than I thought," he chuckled to himself.

"Hang on," he called as the knob twisted back and forth. "You know it's locked." He sighed as he headed down the short hall to the door. "Why are you using the front door anyway? You're not the Avon lady, you know," he automatically needled in response to the sudden unwelcome relief he felt that Lorna was home.

Home? Get a grip or get out of here fast, he told himself, unlocking the front door only three days ago painted the promised radiant blue.

A medium-size man to whom few doors were ever locked stood on the other side. Without invitation or hesitation, he stepped into the house so confidently Julius almost didn't stop him. The spring breeze slammed the front door shut behind the man, the sound bringing Julius back to his senses. He stepped toward the man, preventing him from coming farther inside.

"You know who I am?" The man's voice dominated the small hall.

Because of Lorna's height and the man's reputation, Julius had expected "the Boss" to be a bigger man. Still he had learned long ago a man's power had nothing to do with physical size.

"Your daughter's not home," he told him.

"It's not my daughter I'm here to see."

Julius heard the threat in the man's voice, met the contempt in his eyes, the same gray-green color as Lorna's, only much harder—gray steel, green granite. He felt inside the anger once so familiar, now subdued so long beneath laughter and good times and the freedom to come and go as he pleased. The anger that frightened him as much as anyone who'd been witness to it. He wanted to get away from this man. He didn't move.

"I know about you, boy—what you are and what you did."

Julius kept his face expressionless. Over a month had gone by this time. It was longer than some.

LORNA WAS ONLY A FEW MILES from the farm when the shiny Lincoln had passed her going in the opposite direction. Only one person in Hope owned a Lincoln. She'd turned her own car around. As soon as she rounded the bend and saw the vehicle in her driveway, her first thought was hope. Then she'd laughed out loud—a sad, disparaging laugh.

All this time, and she was still that little girl wanting to please a man who had barely been able to look at her, let alone love her, her very presence only reminding him of what he'd lost.

She pulled into the driveway and parked beside the car the color of black pearls. Her father had come to the farm. To her farm, she thought a little wildly. She parked and hurried inside the house. She was still that little girl.

Both men heard the back door open, but neither shifted his gaze from the other. Lorna came into the hall through the kitchen, saw Julius and her father squared off.

"What a surprise."

Julius glanced over at her, saw the helplessness in her eyes, the helplessness she'd be so angry if she knew it showed. He looked away.

"I see you two have met. Shall we all go into the kitchen?" She was the perfect hostess. "I decided to pass on lunch with the Aunties after all, so just let me put out a few plates and we can all eat together now." She turned to lead the way.

"You know how to pick 'em, Lorna. I'll give you that."

She stopped, her back to her father. Axel's gaze

stayed fast on Julius. "First, a husband who can't keep his pants zipped, then—"

Lorna faced the men. "Mr. Holt is my employee." She willed a note of strength into her voice. "No more."

Axel's gaze swung to his daughter. "He's more, much more." His gaze moved back, sharp on Julius again. "Done a lot of things, haven't you, boy?"

Like a heartbeat, so natural, immediate, Julius felt the physical urge to shove his fist into the man's well-fed face. He breathed. Cool sweat beaded along the back of his neck and under his arms as he wrestled for control. "Yes, sir." His cool, polite response sought to bring the illusion of control he so desperately needed.

"When Mr. Holt applied for the position," Lorna told her father, "he shared with me his various past work experience which included an impressive—"

"He killed a man with his bare hands at sixteen." Axel let a beat of silence fall. "He'd probably still be behind bars today if he hadn't been so young." Such satisfaction in that voice. "I don't suppose that was included on his résumé?"

Julius couldn't look at her. He looked toward the front door she'd painted only three days ago the extraordinary blue. The front door that had let this man in.

"Of course I knew that," Lorna said with such calm conviction, Julius himself almost believed it.

He felt a surge of hope, then felt the fool, knowing her false answer was only for her father's benefit.

"You'll stay for lunch?" Lorna asked her father with the same equanimity.

Axel's voice was low, a man who rarely had to raise his voice to have his words listened to. "You were lucky with your first mistake. The marriage was over soon enough and little was lost except a sizable portion of your trust, and the McDonoughs were temporarily the laughingstock of the community, but I blame myself for sheltering you. It's only natural you'd let someone take advantage of you. Make a mistake once, and you're human. Make the same mistake twice and you're a fool. Fortune doesn't suffer fools, Lorna. And neither do I. Do you understand?"

"Yes, sir." Lorna's expression was as remote as her father's.

Axel nodded, satisfied. "This has gone far enough. You'll come home."

Julius closed his eyes. *It's over.*

"No." From the darkness, he heard Lorna's voice, calm and even, although Julius instinctively knew she wished it stronger. He opened his eyes. She'd tipped her chin. There was no tremble. "You're welcome to join us for lunch."

Such control, Julius wondered, while his own emotions swelled and raged, threatened to overtake him.

Axel's face remained impassive. Only a vein throbbing violently at his temple betrayed him. He stepped toward Lorna. Julius moved, putting his large body between Lorna and her father. The man they called "the Boss" eyed Julius, his expression telling him he'd just made a huge mistake.

Soundlessly Lorna stepped forward and stood beside Julius. "Please join us for lunch."

Axel's scornful gaze fell on his daughter. "You know where your home is." He turned and opened the door.

Lorna watched her father leave, a strength and sadness in her gray-green eyes that made Julius's heart surge.

"Here." She spoke to the empty doorway. "My home is here."

She turned and walked into the kitchen with even steps. But as the wind slammed the front door once more, Julius saw the rail of her spine flinch, and her pain became his. He could look at her no longer. Nor could he move. He stood in the kitchen doorway, waiting for her to tell him to go.

She opened the refrigerator, took a bowl out and set it on the speckled, yellowed counter. "Maybe I'll fry up these leftover mashed potatoes into potato pancakes to go with the chicken." She glanced at him over her shoulder. "You can set the table." Her gaze went to his hands. "After you wash those hands, that is."

He looked down at his hands dirty with the morning's work. Hands that had once taken a man's life. And stripped Julius of the right to sit at any decent person's table for long, least of all someone who, despite all her prickly ways, had fed him fresh bread and given him clean sheets and, with her constant questions and respectful way of watching him work, and her introduction of him as "Mr. Holt" in that well-modulated tone, had made him feel, for a moment, like he was more.

She was lifting the foil off the bowl when she stopped, went still. "Is it true?" she asked.

"Yes."

He waited for her to look at him with disgust or worse, fear in her eyes.

She didn't move for a breath, then she set the foil on the counter, bent and pulled the cast-iron frying pan out from the drawer beneath the stove and set it on a burner. "Go on and get washed up now. I need the table set."

He didn't move, confused by her reaction and his own flush of gratefulness sweet as a woman's kiss. Always, always surprising him, this one. Then he understood, and felt a flash of the anger that he knew always was deep inside him. "I don't need no charity."

She couldn't stop thinking of his hands. Her father had said "killed with his bare hands," and she'd seen those strong, brown hands, dirty now. They'd been her first thought. Those hands that had touched a piece of grass as though it were a jewel, that had led her to a chair after she was sick, that had reached out to a helpless creature such as the runt rabbit…such as herself. Hands that were rebuilding her orchard. She wouldn't let her father take them away. No, not Julius's hands. They were his; they were hers. She thought of the child growing inside her. She needed those hands.

Those thoughts had kept her expression even, her voice calm, and any fear unacknowledged as she'd faced her father and Julius's past. He had already been condemned, yet she could only judge by what she saw. Those hands. The easy laughter, the pretending not to care, the need to come and go, freedom. She understood now.

"I don't need *any* charity," she corrected, briskly moving to the refrigerator and taking out a stick of margarine. She shut the refrigerator door. "And yes, you do, Julius Holt. I don't know anyone, including me or you, who couldn't stand a little charity their way now and then, but that's not what I'm offering you. You were hired here to help with this farm and that's what you've done. I have no complaints nor any reason to ask you to leave."

She stood, facing him, waiting for his response.

"I'll pack up and be moving on as soon as I get this week's wages."

She saw right through him. He'd lived almost his

whole life on the defensive. The carefree, good-time Joe routine was part hunger, part protection. Yet she wasn't going to beg. She squared her shoulders. He had his routine to protect himself…and she had hers. She'd figure out a way to manage until she found help elsewhere. She wouldn't beg him.

She was about to tell him so when his hands lifted and slightly reached toward her. She saw his own surprise as if they didn't belong to him. Her heart swelled as she knew whatever was in him at one time wasn't so strong anymore.

She turned and walked to the stove. Still he didn't move, couldn't move from the sight of her. She glanced at him over her shoulder, her features stern, revealing nothing. Except her eyes, always too honest, and now as soft as the spring all around. He stared at those eyes. He could have swum in those gray-green waters.

Her voice came as strict as the rest of her features. "I asked from you a good day's work and a respect for my land. Nothing more. And so far, that's what you've given me. So, it's your choice, but, if you so decide, you're welcome to stay."

He couldn't remember the last time he'd been welcomed anywhere. Gratefulness came again, sweet and still scary, and he couldn't speak. She turned to the counter. Staring at her stiff back, he stood there a moment more, then turned toward the washroom. He walked quickly, before either one of them could change their minds.

Chapter Six

Julius went into town the next day for supplies and to pick up the roof ordered for the greenhouse. A winter wind had torn away its plastic sheathing, leaving stark ribs in the burgeoning landscape. The snow that had filled the inside had melted to mud, revealing the remains beneath the exposed beams. Lorna was sorting through the pots, plastic trays, heaps of potting mix overturned and scattered by the winds when she heard Aunt Eve's voice. "There she is. Rummaging through the garbage."

"I told you she'd be out here," Aunt Birdy said.

"Did you know she'd be picking through the trash, too?" Aunt Eve asked dryly.

Lorna had expected them. In fact, she'd expected them yesterday once they'd learned of Julius's past. But when afternoon moved into evening and they hadn't arrived, nor had there been a frantic phone call to ascertain their niece hadn't met a ghastly demise at the hands of her handyman, Lorna decided it was only because they hadn't learned of Julius's criminal record yet. Not that she had any doubt they wouldn't. It was only a matter of time before the whole town knew she'd hired an ex-con. *Lorna the Loon,* she thought.

She straightened, a nozzle in one hand, a half-coiled piece of hose in the other. "Aunt Birdy. Aunt Eve." She saw Eve inspecting her waistline. There were shadows beneath Birdy's bright eyes.

"What a nice surprise."

"Hardly," Aunt Eve intoned.

They know, Lorna thought. She leaned in to kiss Birdy's cheek, then straightened to kiss Eve, the taste of their skin against her lips dry and fragile as the kiss itself. Eve studied her figure keenly. They knew about Julius, and they knew about the baby. Lorna braced herself.

Tossing the nozzle onto a pile of objects to be soaked in a weak bleach solution, she looked around the stripped greenhouse. "Lost its roof this past winter." She kept her voice casual. "Julius is in town picking up a new one."

She looked back to Eve's study, Birdy's shadowed eyes. She'd run out of the samples of prenatal vitamins and iron last week and finally filled the prescriptions at the SuperSave, her eyes level with Phyllis, the counter cashier, daring her to ask. Phyllis had handed her the order without a word. Lorna looked at the Aunties. Obviously Phyllis had found her voice.

Lorna placed her hand on her stomach to protect as much as to confirm.

"It's your husband's, I hope?" Eve asked in her autocratic tone.

Less than three months ago, Lorna would have been mortified by such a question. Today she faced Aunt Eve and chuckled, mellowed by the gift within her and so often amused by everything lately in this warm spring sun.

"I know there are some who speculated I might even still be a virgin. I suppose that will lay to rest those rumors."

Birdy rolled her eyes, appealing to the heavens above. "Just when the talk had begun to die down a little."

"You'll come home now." Eve paced the unsheltered greenhouse with the same precise movements Lorna realized she'd inherited. "We'll take care of you."

"No." She answered immediately.

"You need us, Lorna," Birdy said in her thin, high voice. "We're your family. We raised you."

"Yes, you did," Lorna agreed. "And I love you. I love you both, but I've let everyone tell me what to do and take care of me my whole life. It's time I take care of myself."

"We'll move in then," Eve announced.

Oh Lord, Lorna thought. "Aunt Eve, Aunt Birdy, that's so generous, but—"

"You don't want us, Lorna?" Aunt Birdy asked.

"Of course I do," she assured both women. "But somebody's got to take care of my father." Did her father know about the baby? she wondered. She was tempted to ask when she realized it didn't make any difference. If he didn't know, he would soon enough. There were no secrets in Hope from Axel McDonough.

"He's a grown man," Aunt Eve snapped.

"I'm a grown woman."

"He can hire someone to help him."

"But that's what I've already done," Lorna told them.

Eve raised her brows. Birdy gaped at her. Yes, they knew about Julius as well as the baby. Lorna squared her shoulders.

"You have a child to consider now," Aunt Eve said.

"A baby," Birdy chimed in.

"I know, I know. That's why I'm here." She raised her palms up in appeal. "How can I take care of a child, if I can't take care of myself?"

"Here?" Eve folded her arms across her chest as she looked past the stripped steel, the muddy heaps of odds and ends, to the barrels and rusting equipment to the buildings, some plum dilapidated, all in need of paint. Lorna knew what her aunt saw—but Lorna saw only freedom.

Still she felt compelled to defend her decision. "Julius thinks there'll be time to paint after the bloom. And he's got almost all the equipment up and running. He should be back any minute now with the new roof."

Aunt Eve's gaze fell on her niece. "If he doesn't come back and slit your throat first."

Lorna closed her eyes for a quiet second, then opened them to the land, the budding green, the growth and change everywhere around her.

"But, Eve, he does seem like such a nice young man," Birdy said. Lorna turned and looked at her, surprised by the defense. "Very hardworking. And handsome, too." She winked at Lorna, who smiled at her gratefully. "We all make mistakes. And he wasn't much more than a boy when it happened. Maybe we should hear his side of the story before we start bad-mouthing him?"

Eve sent her petite sister a withering look. "He killed a man. You want him sleeping in your backyard?"

Lorna made her voice firm as Aunt Eve's. "Julius is a good employee and has done nothing to give me reason to think otherwise about him."

Eve turned her scornful expression to Lorna. "Good God, he's sweet-talked you, hasn't he? Well, don't expect me to wear chartreuse to your funeral."

"Sweet-talked?"

"Now, Lorna," Birdy attempted to soothe, "he is a rather fetching young man, as I mentioned." Her eyes were dancing again. "And big and strong as they come. And you know how easily you can be swayed."

"'Duped' is the word for it," Eve said.

"No reason to be harsh," Birdy scolded her sister.

Lorna sighed. "I know you both mean well, but I'm happy here." She heard herself say those words for the first time but immediately knew them as true. Even though she wasn't exactly sure of her happiness's source. Maybe it was the sense of her own self fostered by the idea of another human being within her, or the tiredness that came at the end of the day, so complete she slept as if she'd seeded each field with the sweetest hay. Maybe it was watching a dream take shape around her and within her. Whatever it was, she was happy. She stood on her land, faced her aunts and felt strong.

She heard the rumble of wheels coming down the road. Julius.

JULIUS SAW THE WELCOMING ROLL of the land, the recognition moving through him like a warm drink, surprising him. It wasn't until he saw Lorna standing inside the damaged greenhouse, as tall and straight as the naked beams surrounding her, that he realized he'd been looking not only for the land but also for the woman. He drove around back and parked. As he got out of the truck, he saw the aunts, saw the same expressions on their faces as he'd seen in town. Eve's wore a mask of judgment; Birdy's was fear. He told himself it didn't matter. He'd noticed the wary looks and sidelong glances before. He looked at Lorna and saw neither. He was grateful for the respite.

He moved to the truck's bed, hauling out the boxed roof. "Good day, Miss McDonough, Miss McDonough," he said, tipping his head to each lady in turn. He received a stiff nod from Eve, a nervous smile from Birdy. He set the box on the ground.

"You got the roof."

Lorna appeared to be pleased. *That's right, darlin'. Smile, always smile. The hell with the rest of them.* He smiled back. "Even got it at a sale price."

"They're saying you killed a man." Eve's challenge raised a sudden beat of blood in Julius's temple.

"Aunt Eve, you have no right—"

Julius raised his hand, stopping Lorna. "They would be right, ma'am."

"Did you have a reason?" she asked when Julius said nothing more.

"I thought I did at the time." Julius's gaze stayed level with the older woman's.

"But you don't think so now?"

"What I think now is no man has the right to take

another's life.'' He looked at Eve steadily with his full, brilliant blue eyes.

"The man you killed, he was a respected businessman, a well-known member of the community, I understand.''

Julius said nothing.

"Aunt Eve—" Lorna again interrupted.

"Why'd you do it?" Eve asked.

"He hurt someone I knew," Julius answered.

"They said you were robbing his house when he came home unexpectedly, tried to stop you.''

"He hurt someone I knew," Julius repeated flatly. "She thought he loved her. It was two months before her body was found floating in the river. They said it was suicide. She was pregnant. She was fourteen and beautiful.'' He touched the gold medal always around his neck. "She was my sister.''

He waited as if for more questions, but even Eve was silent. He turned. The women watched him walk to the barn and disappear inside. The sun shone and the spring birds sounded and the murmurs of the melted waters rose and the women were silent.

Finally Birdy said, ''He's not a murderer.''

No one answered her, but they all understood.

LORNA WAS SITTING on the stoop in the little light left, sorting bills. She had to squint to read the numbers in the twilight, but she liked to sit here and look at the trees, her trees, dressed all in green as if now, not January, were the new year.

She brought a bill up closer to her face, made out the amount due and released a sigh as she placed it on top of the others. Barring no emergencies, she had enough money to get the farm going and take care of herself and the baby for several years. Surely the farm would be up and running by then. In the meantime, she had to watch costs closely.

Engrossed in figures and balances due, she didn't hear Julius come until he said, "The lower field's planted. I'll get that roof on tomorrow."

She jumped and was immediately sorry. She didn't want him to think she was afraid of him.

"Good night." He turned to go to the trailer.

"Ironic, isn't it?" she said, wanting to hold him there, let him know she wasn't scared of him.

He gave her a quizzical glance.

"Daughter of the richest man in town and here I am, worrying about bills." She smiled.

"The weather's cooperating and the crops will be good," he assured her.

"I know," she agreed, although both knew it was only talk, words to reassure themselves when all was so uncertain.

He turned again to go.

Lorna spoke to his broad back. "I'm sorry about your sister." She had the feeling the girl had been the last thing he'd loved.

He stopped, but it was a few seconds before he turned. When he finally did, he said, "How come you never asked me why I did it?"

She stared at him. "I didn't need to."

He looked at her a minute. "Thank you."

She watched him walk away, a man too alone for too long.

HE UNDRESSED in the new darkness and slipped into bed. Damn. Crisp, smooth sheets. Lorna must have come in today and changed them. He lay on his back, stared up at the stained ceiling and sighed. Clean sheets. A man could be ruined by a woman like that.

He sighed again and turned onto his side, making a fist and plumping the pillow that smelled of the spring wind. He dropped his head into the softness and closed his eyes. And saw Lorna sitting in the young moonlight, her smile tender and her eyes gray and green and gentle. He buried his face deeper into the sweet pillow. Still he saw her as she'd been moments ago.

He rolled onto his other side. He had wanted to kiss her then. He wanted to kiss her now, feel the line of her lips go lax against his; kiss her deep and long until her body lost its natural stiffness and swayed to him.

It was only the night, the night that had painted her and, now, painted his thoughts. Still he knew she was not as she seemed. Few were. Beneath her rigid exterior, there was a woman, soft, sweet, scared. He smiled as he thought of her. She amused him, intrigued him…touched him—a man who'd made an art of becoming untouchable. He thought of her now in her own bed. Did she turn and toss as he did, the cool rub of fresh linen touching…touching everywhere?

He rolled onto his back, another sigh releasing. He couldn't afford to care…neither could she. Both had worked so hard to go beyond that. He closed his eyes, saw her face, remembered how her eyes had softened when he thanked her. And he knew what he'd probably always known—no man moves past the caring.

He pushed away the sheets and sat up. He needed a drink, noise, the blank, almost professional gaze of a woman who wanted no more than he did—a hot night, a warm body and the chance to forget.

THE SMELLS OF SMOKE and sweat and sweet cologne greeted him even before he pulled open the tavern's door. He stepped inside and looked around the dim rooms, the U-shaped bar. He'd been away too long. He walked to an empty space at the bar but didn't sit. The glances were more curious and bold than wary. Liquor had left little wariness.

"Beer with a Jack back," he told the bartender as she came over and leaned toward him, the low vee of her shirt beckoning to a pair of full, creamy breasts. She brought him his drinks. He looked her full in the eye, saw her youthful look was more makeup and dim lights than reality. He threw back his shot and waited for its warmth. He hadn't come here for reality.

The bartender brought his change, smiled. "New in town?"

Julius pushed the empty shot glass toward the edge of the bar, threw some bills beside it and smiled. "As the day's beginning."

She smiled a little wider, reached for the liquor bottle behind her and filled his glass. Smiles were easy in a place like this, as were tears. "So, what brings you to Hope?"

Hope. He saw Lorna's face. He picked up the shot glass, drank. Lorna's image dissolved. "The question is what would make me stay?" He smiled, his eyes lingering on the woman's face.

The woman returned his smile.

"Hey, Tina, what's a man got to do to get a drink around here?" a man called from the other end of the bar.

"Nothing," she answered, her gaze and smile still on Julius. Her voice lower, she added, "All he's got to do is tell me what he wants."

Julius watched her walk away. He waited for the pleasure that always came from drink and dimness and desire. All that came was the thought that it was noisy in here. The laughter was too loud, the songs he'd heard all before, the smoke was choking and the smells cheap. He looked around to anonymous faces, anonymous expressions. In the mirror behind the bar, he saw the same anonymous expression on his own face. He took a pull from his beer bottle and looked away. In his mind's eye, he saw Lorna's disapproving frown. *None of your business,* he told her. But he knew it was—he had to get up at four tomorrow. He had to finish fertilizing the north end, see about leasing some hives for bloom and, hell, Lorna had told him tonight at supper she wanted to learn to drive the tractor and he was going to teach her.

He chuckled at the thought, then just as quickly, his smile fell away and he reached for his beer bottle. He took another long pull and wiped his mouth on his sleeve, defying the thought of Lorna once more.

What the hell was happening to him? A little over a month on a farm more destined for failure than success with a woman wound tighter than a corkscrew, two old-maid aunts convinced he was Jack the Ripper and a father who, Julius knew, could cause him as much trouble in this town as he wanted. And he not even able to enjoy a man's simple pleasure of a slow drunk and a woman's smile, which he knew from experience got prettier until morning.

Damn, he'd promised himself he wouldn't let it happen again, wouldn't let himself care about anyone or anything again. Now it was too late. A crazy schoolmarm and the promise of more had gotten under his skin.

He hadn't been able to save his sister. Not his father. Not his mother. Not the man who'd hit his head and cracked his skull when Julius attacked him. What made him think this time was different? What made him think he could make a difference to a failing farm and its eccentric owner?

Lorna did. The thought came without hesitation. She believed in the farm's success; she believed in him. No one had ever believed in him before.

Poor, naive Lorna. How could she believe in him when he'd let everyone else down in the past? Damn caring. He should've left when he had the chance. He'd leave tomorrow, he told himself. He'd leave right now. Damn caring. He got up, leaving his half-full beer and a few singles on the bar. Damn caring.

"Where you going, cowboy?" The bartender came back, smiling in invitation.

The answer rose and was out of his mouth before he even thought about it. "Home."

The truth stunned him. He was getting out of Hope not a minute too soon.

He was halfway to the farm, past the outlying new developments to the darkness of only land and sky and the occasional house spaced far from any other, when he saw the police car's strobelike blue-and-red lights, even brighter in the total night, signaling him to pull over.

LORNA CHECKED the clock. Five-thirty. She scraped the cold scrambled eggs and toast into the garbage can and again looked out the window to the backyard as she placed the plate in the sink. *He's gone*. The thought seemed to pierce her to the bone. *He's gone*.

Nonsense. He probably overslept, she thought, welcoming anger and annoyance over any other emotions as she headed out the back door and across the lawn to the trailer.

She didn't hesitate until she got to the door. Chiding herself, she swung it open and marched down the hall to the bedroom only to be embarrassed by the relief that swept through her when she saw his blanketed back turned toward her.

"I'm not cooking another breakfast. You'll have to wait until lunch now." She moved into the room, clapping her hands. Her gaze fell on the opened duffel bag beside the dresser. He had never even unpacked. She moved to the bedside, clapped hard above his head. She thought she heard a moan. She stopped, waited, but the blanketed form didn't move.

"C'mon, stop faking it," she said half in taunt, half in fear. She shook his shoulder. "Julius?"

Another low moan escaped as he turned slowly toward her. She stepped back and gasped as she saw his swollen, bruised face. "What happened? Who did this to you?"

She suspected the answer even as she asked the question.

"We've got to get you to a doctor."

He shook his head. "I'm fine," he said in a low, dry voice. "Maybe not as pretty..." He attempted a smile, grimaced. "But I'm fine." He rolled back on his side away from her.

"The hell you are." She looked at his bruised profile. Anger and frustration swelled inside her. She was as much to blame for those bruises as if she'd landed the blows herself.

"C'mon." She drew the covers off his shoulder, saw the black and blue flesh. "Doc Tierney is an old family friend. I'll give him a call and have him take a look at you."

When he didn't move, she gently laid her hand on his shoulder. "He gives a lollipop to every patient who needs a shot, and I'll hold your hand if you need stitches."

He slowly rolled toward her. She smiled down at him encouragingly, trying to hide the frustration and anger still within her.

"What'll you hold if it's really serious?" He wiggled his eyebrows and again tried to smile.

"I see your sparkling wit wasn't injured." She looked down at his discolored, distorted face, the gaping cut on his brow. Feeling as if her heart would break, she reached out and smoothed the hair carefully off his forehead in such an unconscious gesture of caring, her hand lingered for a moment before she realized the inappropriateness of her touch. She pulled her hand back. Still her gaze met his. Neither looked away for a long minute until she felt the tears come into her eyes. She turned away.

"Lorna." It was he who touched her now with just the hush of his voice. "It's only a few bumps and bruises. I've looked worse after a long weekend in Atlantic City."

She shook her head. "It's my fault. My father…"

"You don't know that."

She looked at him. "He's used to people doing as he says and when they don't…" Again her voice trailed off.

"Nah, it was just a full moon, Lorna. I myself had an itch that needed scratching and ended up at Monk's Tavern, doing shots of Captain Jack and flirting with the barmaid. On the way home, I saw some flashing lights behind me, and well, let's just say, it wasn't the welcoming committee." He smiled a half smile. "I guess a good time was had by all."

She looked down at him, her face still grave. Her voice went soft. "You don't have to pretend with me, Julius. You know that, don't you? You don't have to pretend for me. You're hurt, and I want to help you. Please let me."

Every defense inside him crumbled. He'd had no one for so long—no one who had thought any more of him than what they had been told; no one who he'd cared to try to make think otherwise. No one. Until Lorna.

Silently he nodded. She took a half step back, and he feared the gratefulness had overwhelmed his expression, showed in his eyes and scared her.

"Can you get dressed?"

"What are you going to do if I can't?" He smiled, breaking the tension.

She eyed him. "Well, I suppose you'll be the first patient Doc Tierney has ever seen wearing a toga."

"In that case, I do believe I can manage a pair of pants and a shirt."

"I never doubted it." She turned on her heel and walked smartly out the room. It wasn't until she was outside and around the corner that she let her body sag against the side of the building as intense, unexpected emotions assaulted her. Desire, fear, desperation, need.

It hadn't been like this before, she thought. What she'd experienced with her late husband didn't even come close. It had never been so primitive, so elemental. It was more than sheer attraction.

Lorna forced herself to straighten. After all that had happened, was she so pathetic, so lonely, she'd forgotten how false feelings can be, how easily emotions can cloud clear judgment?

Yet she'd seen it in Julius's eyes, too. Just as quickly she dismissed the thought, certain it'd only been a reflection of her own desire.

She walked to the house. Her strong reaction had been fueled by guilt. She knew her father had a hand in what happened last night, as he did in most everything that went on in Hope. Not that he'd actually issued an order to have Julius roughed up or anything quite so crass. Yet she was sure he took it upon himself to remind the local police chief, who was up for re-election in the fall, it was his job to protect the good people of this town and keep the streets of Hope safe from the threat of dangerous elements.

Along with the guilt, the fact that hormones had flooded her body, were constantly coursing through her veins, turning her emotional equilibrium and libido every which way, certainly didn't help the situation.

By the time she reached the house, she felt better. She climbed the back steps, calm and in control, having determined the sources of her sudden, overwhelming feelings. They were, after all, nothing more than the products of every woman's curse—guilt and hormones.

Chapter Seven

Lorna burst through the conference room door, ignoring the curious gazes. "Leave him alone," she said to the man seated at the head of the table.

She continued toward her father, her fists clenched as she again thought of the three cracked ribs and the stitches above his left eye Julius had received that morning.

"Leave him alone," she said, the McDonough blood that had made millionaires of Scottish immigrants with little more than the clothes on their back and the dream in their heart running in her veins.

Her father peered at her over his half glasses, removed them, looked to his executives without apology. "Gentlemen," was all he said.

The men rose and filed out of the room. They didn't look at Lorna.

Her father waited until the last man was gone, the door closed behind him. He looked at his daughter.

"How dare you." He was a man who never had to raise his voice. When he did, it was terrifying.

She thought of Julius bloodied and bruised. She thought of her child and made her legs stand strong, and ignored the tremble inside her.

"Why'd you have to do it? Why'd you have to hurt him?"

He stared at her. "Is it true? Are you pregnant?"

She understood. It wasn't a matter of control now. It was the fact of her child—his grandchild. And, just as she feared, when her father wanted something, he would go to any lengths to get it.

"I would never keep my child from his grandfather."

Something flickered in her father's eyes, something deep and rarely seen, an unknown, pure emotion. "So it is true." His voice was normal volume. The fury had left as swiftly as it had risen, taking away the monster and leaving only a man.

"I didn't know until after the funeral. The baby's due the last week in October."

"Come home, Lorna."

There was a note of honest plea. She stared at her father. "I have to make my own life."

"I'm trying to save you from ruining your life."

"My employee was stopped by the local patrol last night and told his type wasn't welcome in Hope. Then they proceeded to give him a demonstration. Was that for my salvation? Or his?"

Her father eyed her levelly. "From what I hear, he got himself into a brawl in Monk's parking lot."

"There was no brawl in Monk's lot. There was an ambush outside of town." Emotion crept into her voice. "He hadn't even done anything wrong."

"The man's a criminal."

"He made a mistake. He did his time. We all make mistakes."

"So true," her father said pointedly. She knew he was referring to her first marriage.

"That doesn't mean we can't change."

"Have you changed, Lorna? Looks to me like you're still falling for any line that's fed you."

"Julius is my employee. That's it." She denied the attraction there almost from the beginning, the friendship that had developed since.

She saw the skepticism on her father's face. "Leave him alone."

"Trouble seems to follow that boy." She heard the threat. "I can't control that."

"Very little goes on in Hope that you don't control." She swallowed hard but kept her gaze steady on him. "Including my late husband's death."

Axel steepled his fingers and stared at his daughter. "Are you accusing your father of murder, Lorna?"

"I don't think you ever expected it to go that far."

"As I recall, it was your husband who broke the Sixth Commandment." Her father adopted the tone of a reasonable, patient man. "Some simply say justice was done. Now your hired hand, he broke the Fifth, I believe—'Thou shalt not kill.' Is that correct?"

She again heard the threat. "Leave Julius Holt alone."

She walked out of the room, took the elevator to the main floor and walked out into the spring sunshine. Her steps were steady down the sidewalk, across the street to the town square. It wasn't until she reached the bench that her legs buckled and she had to sit, her head lowered to her knees until the wave of nausea passed.

"Ow, WATCH IT! What is that stuff anyway? Turpentine?"

"Stop being such a baby," Lorna told Julius as she dabbed the cotton ball over his left brow. "That's all we need—an infection."

"'We'?" Julius eyed her. "I'm the one sitting here being put into pain."

"Well, I'm the one who has to listen to it, so be quiet."

"Regular Florence Nightingale, you are."

She was about to retort when his gaze lifted, met hers and he smiled, his face so close, so handsome even with its blacks and blues, that she wanted to open her palm and touch his cheek.

His smile drained and, for a moment, there was only each other.

She stepped back to break the spell. She picked up the cotton balls and the bottle of antiseptic. "That ought to do it." She walked smartly to the narrow cupboard where she kept the aspirin and thermometer and her prenatal vitamins and iron tablets. She put away the bottle and bag of cotton balls and shut the cupboard.

"Unless you need to torture me further, I'm off to the orchard to check the bloom."

"Julius?" She stopped him as he reached the door.

He glanced at her over his shoulder. "Don't tell me. You've found a new way to cause me pain." He saw her grave face. His own expression sobered.

"I think you should leave," she said.

It was like a blow from behind. Never mind it was the same decision he'd made last night, but that was before he'd met up with the town's welcoming committee. Frightened by his own feelings, he'd been ready to run, but he'd be damned if he'd let someone run him off again. Afraid of his own temper and strength, he'd walked away from many a fight. Even last night, he'd landed no blows. He looked out to the land, back to Lorna. But then again, since his sister's death, he hadn't had anything worth fighting for.

"You want me to leave?" He kept his expression neutral.

Her eyes, those honest, honest eyes suddenly filled with sadness. She shook her head. "I need you."

Her words filled him. Such strength—to be needed, to be wanted, to be necessary.

"But I'm afraid..." She sat down as if weary, stared at the table, the sadness spreading across her features. "I'm afraid something might happen to you."

"What're you talking about?" He made his voice hearty to take away her sadness. "Nothing's going to happen to me."

She looked up at him. The sadness was still there although she smiled an ironic smile. "Have you looked in the mirror lately?"

He moved to the table, yanked a chair out and turning it around then straddled it. "Chicks dig scars, believe me."

The smile became sad. "Not this chick." Her gaze went to the stitches across his brow. Her hand lifted as if she wanted to touch the wound. He remembered the sweetness of her touch this morning when all else was pain. He wanted her to touch him again. He wanted to touch her. Her hand hovered a few inches above her thigh. He reached for it, took it in his. She didn't pull away.

"Lorna, nothing's going to happen to me."

He sat in the angle of the sun, the light bathing every detail of his face, swollen, bruised and still beautiful. She lifted her other hand, driven by an instinct elemental and old as the world, and opened her palm gently to his cheek. He placed his hand on her forearm as if to pull it away, but then his fingers only slid, circled her wrist as he turned his face into her palm, kissed its tender center.

Her fingers reached, brushed the dark curls that framed his face and fell long on his neck. He closed his eyes as if they might reveal something more than laughter or mischief, something he didn't want her to see.

She leaned toward him, tenderly tasted his cheek, felt the bristle of beard against her lips, heard the breath released from deep within him. Her mouth moved to his temple, lightly near the fresh, angry stitches. Her lips slid across his brow, rested against the pulse of blood in his temple. She grazed the side of his face once more. Her lips found his and kissed them with the sweetest of kisses.

He felt nothing—no pain, no ache, nothing but her lips. She tasted like tomorrow, all the tomorrows he'd once dreamed of. He had to stop kissing her. A kiss was too intimate, too needy, but his fingers circled her wrist and held on. Then he heard her sigh of sweet promise and he drank to become drunk with her, pulling her up out of the chair and her body to his. Her hands tangled in his hair. She angled her head, opened her mouth, giving, holding him as if to never let go. The kiss became a movement of its own, the easy rhythm of their tongues touching, the richness of the taste, the stretch of a sigh as if coming awake slowly. The dance built, mounted. The muscles tensed, and for the first time, Julius felt himself tumbling, falling, flailing, searching for the way home.

He pulled away, the separation ripping through him, scaring him further. He had been with many women, women who took as well as they gave and were satisfied. He stepped back from Lorna. She stood very still as if about to shatter. He didn't want to care about anyone. He knew about the baseness within him, within others, the darkness that came, had killed his sister, had clamped his own hands around a man's neck. He knew evil. He knew little of love.

Lorna had caught the fear before his expression had closed down. So quickly it came; just as quickly it was concealed. There'd been no contempt or derision as she'd seen in her late husband's gaze. Julius was simply afraid. As was she.

"Well…well, well, well." She decided to be brave for the both of them. "Now that we got that out of the way, maybe it's time we got some work done around here."

She never failed to surprise. The tenderness welled up within him. She was right. He should leave. As tough as she pretended to be, she was that tender underneath. And, in the end, he would hurt her. Even if he could stay and love her, Lorna deserved better than him, better than a man who had killed another. His past couldn't be changed; his sins would only cause her suffering. He didn't want to hurt her. He didn't want to get hurt.

"You're right," he told her. "It's time I'm moving on."

She saw the fear flicker in his eyes once more, then disappear. What scared him—that she would say yes and ag————————————————— ———— ——— ——— — stay?

"I'll go after the bloom. The pickers will be coming into Laurel soon for the season. I'll make the trip find you two good men before I go. They'll bring in their brothers or cousins come harvest. In the meantime, I'll teach you to train the branches and thin the fruit."

She listened, watching his face. What did he really want? To stay or go? How could she know when she didn't even know what she wanted anymore? All she knew was she didn't want to cause this man more pain.

He'd finished and was waiting for her to speak.

"You have to teach me to drive the tractor before you go."

He nodded. "About..." His hands wavered in the air as he searched for the words.

No more pain, she thought. "That was lovely." She smiled. "But, after all, it was only a kiss," she lied.

He looked at her. "You're quite a woman, Lorna."

"Flatter me all you want. It's not going to get you out of planting the far field before you go either."

He smiled, giving her pleasure. "You can dish it out but you can't take it, can you?"

"I can take plenty. Go on with you now."

At the door, he turned. "Lorna?"

She gave an exasperated sigh. "What?"

"I meant what I said."

He crossed the backyard and disappeared into the

the box beside the stove. The rabbit was almos enough to release in the woods soon. She picked up the animal, stroked his velvet fur, needing to touch something soft and warm and alive, as if to remember how she'd been made to feel moments ago.

She raised the bunny, rubbed her nose to his. "You're my witness," she told the furry creature. "You heard him say it, too. 'You're quite a woman, Lorna.'"

Funny, she thought as she placed the bunny back in his box—no one had ever realized it, not even herself, until this moment.

MAYBE IT WAS BECAUSE he would soon be leaving, eliminating any complications that could arise. Maybe it was the heady freedom that came with her vow to never again marry. Maybe it was the sheer proximity of him, his strength, his surprising size, the seductive flash of his smile. Maybe it was nothing more than hormones. Maybe she didn't even need a reason except she wanted him.

It had begun before the kiss, but after, there was no denying her desire. She grew fascinated with him—the width of his hands, the thickness of his fingers, the sturdy curve of his shoulder. For too long she would study his face, the blue eyes that always startled her, the broad cheekbones, the hard chin, until he slowly swung his gaze to her. Even then, she'd last three seconds more before she looked away, leaving him amused.

She was fascinated by him…as she was fascinated by herself, the changes in her body known only to her—the rounding of her stomach so that it fit perfectly in the curve of her hands, the new fullness in her breasts, her hips, so that she walked with more of a sway and her chest thrust proudly.

She was tall with a long torso, and wide hips, so there had been no more than a gradual softening, a playful push of her belly, her breasts, her thighs. The morning sickness had passed at the beginning of her fifth month, her appetite hearty, and she was ten pounds above her slight weight, a ten pounds her frame carried without comment.

She dreamed of the day she would first feel movement in her womb, and she ate like a truck driver, feeding herself, her child. She worked tirelessly, everything new and amazing and the work never done. She would work from sunrise to sunset, pacing herself while the grooves of her fingers filled with dirt and the ground was tilled and the weeds rampaged and words like *fruit set, cross-pollination* and *spray schedules* were part of everyday conversation. Come night, too tired to move off the stoop where she'd dropped to watch the pines darken, she'd admire the blossoming rows of apple trees and imagine her child running through the rows to the fields not yet cultivated; her child running through the tall grass and weeds and wildflowers—free as the eye of the wind.

She'd sit past dark and think of Julius. She wanted to love like a man, lay down with another for no more reason than pleasure, no more cause than it could be done. It was the sense of life within her and all around her; it was an awakened need that had made her vulnerable to her late husband's lies; it was elevated hormone levels and longer, warmer days and the feel of her hair soft across her back and her brightly, boldly colored house and a million other sights and sensations that made her thoughts of sex. Simple, hot, no-holds-barred pleasure for no other reason than the celebration of it.

She had no need of marriage. She had defied her father, been made a fool by her late husband, freed by the entire experience and given the gift of a child and this sweet, sweet land. It might have been she who had used her late husband. Surely she'd become the victorious one.

And so she stepped triumphant, as if she'd already spread her strong thighs and felt Julius's thrust within her and herself crying out. Yes, she would cry out, a sweet scream of sheer celebration as her womb, heavy with child, filled even fuller with this man, then as easily released him, letting him smile and herself, powerful, newborn, autonomous, laughed out loud.

The days grew less until he would leave. He taught her the things he'd promised—how to train the branches to the correct angle by tying weights or fashioning a homemade spreader by partially pounding nails into each end of a wooden lath and cutting the heads off the nails; how the largest central apple blossom was called the ''king'' and produced the largest apples. The temperatures stayed above sixty degrees and the rain was adequate and the wind mild, as if even the universe at large agreed with Lorna's endeavors. She learned to tie silver strips to the branches and flap her arms and mutter and swear at the birds, although there was little else that could be done to prevent their damage to the trees. In preparation for his leaving, she learned everything Julius could teach her. And she waited, readying herself as she touched her inner thighs, the dark centers of her full, proud breasts, the base of her stomach where the skin had begun to stretch, swelling with all the life within her. She had decided. Before Julius left, she would ask him to teach her one more lesson.

"I heard the owner of Valley View Orchards talking at Field's today. He's looking to buy a good, used tractor," Julius told her as he came into the kitchen for supper one night. "The money from the John Deere could help pay for an extra man."

"And what am I supposed to use for a tractor?" she asked, standing at the stove, stirring the gravy. "A mule?"

He smiled. "No, we don't need any more stubbornness around here." He had washed up. His hair lay damp and dark and relaxed across his thick neck. He went to the refrigerator, took out the carton of milk and brought it to the table. "I got the older one, the Massey Ferguson in the far barn back together and running. It'll do you just as good."

"I'll bet it's not as pretty," she said, carrying a bowl of beans to the table.

He poured a glass of milk. "Prettier than an orchard full of rotting apples, which is what you'll have without a proper picking crew."

She brought the rest of the food to the table. They were silent as they filled their plates, the day's long light filling the room.

"Where will you go when you leave here?" Lorna asked, breaking the comfortable silence. No date had been set, and since that night, that kiss, they'd only referred to his leaving in vague terms. They referred to the kiss not at all.

He shrugged and reached for a roll. "Haven't given it much thought, to tell you the truth."

"You just get up and go?"

"Pretty much," he said through a mouthful of mashed potatoes.

"Don't talk with your mouth full," she scolded.

"Then don't ask me questions while I'm eating," he told her.

She raised a brow, but then smiled.

He smiled back. "Makes sense, don't it?"

She looked down at her plate, still smiling. Everything seemed to make sense lately, even though it shouldn't. She was unmarried, with the child of a man who'd never loved her, living with a drifter soon to leave her on a farm more ready for failure than success, and she was happy. Lord knows why. She didn't even care. She was just going to hold on to it as long as possible.

"Tell me where you've been," she asked him.

So he did. He told her how the full moon turned pale as it rose above the Pacific Ocean and the white trim of the houses facing the sea shimmered in the light; how the tumbleweeds chased one another across the Midwest fields as if in a game of tag and the long sweeps of redtop and timothy lay down beneath the wind like an inland sea while the grasses sang a calming song. For her, he made it magical—

this woman who listened, her chin cupped in her hands. And in her strange eyes, he saw it was a wondrous world.

"You should take a trip, travel," he told her.

She smiled, her chin still cupped in her hands as she nodded slowly. "Perhaps I will." But then she looked past him to the window and the land beyond and he knew she'd never really leave. Just as she'd known he wouldn't stay.

Supper was over, but both were slow to rise from their chairs.

"Aw, go on," he said with a teasing lilt, "another year or two, you'll be married and making babies."

She looked at him, the shine still in her eyes and the smile on her lips, turning a plain face beautiful. "No, I won't marry again."

"No?" He leaned back in his chair, incredulous. "Well, sure you will."

"Why?" Her smile teased him now.

"Because that's what you women want."

Her head tipped back slightly as she softly laughed. "Not this woman."

"Now Lorna—" he saw her eyes soften as he said her name "—don't let some miserable excuse for a man like your first husband ruin you."

"He didn't ruin me," she said so earnestly Julius had to agree. "Actually, in the long run, marrying him was the one of the smartest things I've ever done." She looked startled, as if the confession surprised even her, but then she explained, "If he hadn't come along and told me he loved me and if I hadn't been such a fool and believed him, I'd probably have spent the rest of my days doing what my father said was best, trying to make him happy. And, when all's said and done, I'm afraid my late husband got the brunt end of the deal. Now some will tell you in town I'm still acting like a fool, and maybe I am, but you know what, Julius Holt? These last few months, here on this farm, my farm—" she spread her arms and smiled wide "—I'm a gloriously happy fool."

He shook his head as he chuckled softly. "You sure are something, Miss Lorna, but nothing I've quite figured out yet."

"I'm taking that as a compliment." She tilted her head, a self-satisfied smile on her face. Julius couldn't remember ever seeing a woman more grand.

"So, why won't you marry?"

"Why won't you?" The smug smile remained.

He had seen many instances of man's evil to another. What he hadn't seen was love. "Don't believe in it, that's all. Not for a guy like me." A man with another man's blood on his hands. Did she think of his sins also? From the small smile still charming her face he didn't think so. He questioned why it even mattered.

She looked at him thoughtfully, the slight smile still there. The room's light had lowered, turned as thoughtful as the woman opposite him. Still there was enough light to check the nozzles on the irrigation pipe. He pushed back from the table.

"There is something I do want though," Lorna said as he rose, her voice as thoughtful as her expression.

Julius looked down at her in the pearl dusk.

She raised her head to him. "I would like you to teach me the pleasures of lovemaking."

Chapter Eight

He sank back down into the chair as if needing support.

She mugged an expression of *Oops!* "Took you by surprise there, huh?"

Always, he thought. Aloud, he said, "Your husband...he didn't..."

"He did, yes, but his idea of lovemaking..." Her face became solemn. "I don't mean to speak ill of the dead, but I must say, if that was what he considered great sex, I'm surprised the woman he was sleeping with didn't shoot him before her husband."

His smile was a slow curve. It broadened into a soft chuckle, a velvety sound that made Lorna swallow hard and wonder how she had dared to ask such a thing of any man...of this man. Still she kept her chin proudly raised and her gaze constant on this man she'd just asked to make love to her. Funny thing was, here, her body flowering with life and the farm breaking into bloom, her request seemed only one more natural act in a sequence of life and death and anger and lust and love. As natural as the bees flitting from blossom to blossom, bringing life to what otherwise would remain sterile, wither and die.

She laid her hand on the slight mound of her stomach. She didn't want to go back to what she'd been before—alone, sterile, afraid. It didn't have to be love. She'd waited so long for love, she'd fallen for the first man who'd professed it—she was that hungry. No, she didn't want love. She wanted fulfillment. She wanted to feel the physical pleasure so tauntingly promised by her late husband but never delivered. She wanted to satisfy the yearning she had either denied or dreamed about for so long. Her desire, awoken, would no longer sleep.

"Lorna."

She heard her name in his breath, and she wasn't sorry she'd asked him. She looked into those wicked blue eyes. She was scared, scared to death. But she wasn't sorry.

Those blue eyes stayed steady on her. "That's not what you want."

"It is." Her answer was calm; her stare brave. Yet she couldn't eliminate her hesitation when she asked, "Do you want me?"

Surprise again flashed in his eyes and was followed by his velvet chuckle once more. But when he spoke, the laughter wasn't in his eyes. "I'm not what you want."

She looked at the man opposite her. The man who'd taught her to sift the dirt between her fingers and knead it with her toes, to celebrate the sun and the soil and the ache of a long, hard day's work. The man who tilled her land as if he had finally come home; who touched the bleeding end of a new-pruned limb as if he too were in pain. He would never tell her he loved her, would never promise to stay, and had made aggravating her into a high art form. He had taught her to laugh. She saw the best friend she'd ever had.

She looked into his eyes that hid everything. "You're everything I need."

If he was a man who gave his heart away, he would have given it to her right then, forever. But he'd learned long ago to keep his heart his own. He stood. He knew she deserved more. He would give her everything else.

She rose to meet him as if as brave and certain as he pretended to be. She didn't know her eyes never lied. He saw her vulnerability, felt it inside him with clutching awareness. She stood in the dusk, beautiful and fragile. He couldn't touch her. Not with these hands. These soiled hands that would hold her, then too easily, push her away. He didn't want to hurt her. He had promised himself. He would cause no more pain.

"Lorna."

As she heard the decision in his voice, her eyes filled and darkened. He had brought her pain after all. He murmured her name even softer to soothe her. The need to comfort her rose.

"I'm leaving soon."

"I never expected otherwise," she said in her familiar flat tone, but when she spoke again, her voice shook. "For one night, one moment..." Her eyes, those gray-green waters, washed over him. "I don't want to be alone anymore."

The words spoken in her trembling tone hit him like a blow to the gut, a pain that would double over most men.

"I know I'm not beautiful—"

"You're wrong." He tightened his hands into fists at his sides to stop from touching her.

She wet her lips. "Make love to me, Julius."

She spoke her plea as if he were a noble man, not a man who'd killed another. He looked to his fisted hands, hands that didn't deserve to touch a woman like her.

"This isn't what you want, Lorna."

She stepped closer. He could smell the pure scent of soap and sweetness. She was close enough to touch. One step closer, and she'd be close enough to kiss. She looked up boldly, but her words were no more than a whisper. "Do you want me, Julius?"

Lie was his first thought. He gazed into those eyes.

Hadn't he known at first glance they'd be the death of him? He cursed their clear, delicate honesty even now as he fell into them. His lips found her, the taste even sweeter than he remembered. She opened her mouth, welcoming him. There would be no going back now. Hell, he'd never had any luck being the hero anyway.

As his lips touched hers, the size of him, the sense of him took away all Lorna's fears. She needed only the sheer strength and solidity of him surrounding her. His mouth was so wonderfully hard and hot, yet the wide width of his palm lightly touched the small of her back as if she were precious. When his mouth pulled back, she rose on tiptoes, her lips clinging, reluctant to let go. She heard his rumble of amusement as he pressed his rough, raw cheek to hers. His breath rose hard from his lungs. They stood together for a moment, bodies pressed, she holding her own breath.

His lips came back to her, the kiss turning slow and easy and long as if they were sleeping in a most delicious dream. His hand played upon the curve of her broadening waist, brushed the new fullness of her breast, found her face to trace her cheek still moist from his mouth. She remembered how he'd touched a blade of grass that first day he came, the way he'd held it as if he had to. She felt as singularly rare and wondrous.

Her hands still tight on his strong, full shoulders,

she took a step back and smiled at him. His expression was both lost and found. She dropped her hands to the wide planes of his back, following its rich slope as if to warm him, he all the time studying her; she all the time smiling.

"Take me to your bedroom."

His strong voice, the dark glaze of his eyes sent a tremble of excitement through her. She took his hand in hers and led him down the narrow hall, up the steep stairs to a half-opened door at the end. She saw the room's sparseness and vowed to paint its walls lemon and to sew curtains of gay stripes hung on wide, shiny ribbons. Yet through the twin windows, she saw the darkening lay of the land greeting the coming night. She turned to Julius. He looked to the land, too. He pulled her into his arms, kissing her with a passion that made her body feel hot and full and needy. Needing him.

He led her to the bed, easing her down, leaning over to kiss her cheekbones. His fingers found the buttons of her shirt, undid them one kiss at a time while the deep longing within her took form. Her body filled with rich sensations, an ache so deep with desire, she could do no more than twine her hands around his neck and hang on. She might have been a virgin, so new was each sensation, each breath of intense, awakening sensuality. It hadn't been like this with her husband. No, so different now with Julius, she wanted to weep. She wanted to laugh. She wanted to explore each new, rippling thrill moving through her now. Life, she thought. That is what this is. Life and more. Shame on her husband for denying her this. Her fingers circled Julius's wrist, pulled his wide, rough hand to her breast and, rising to meet him, took his mouth and drank deeply of life with a passion as frightening as it was thrilling.

"It wasn't like this," she said again and again, not in a whisper.

"Then shame on him—your husband," Julius told her, echoing her own thought completely, then laughing deeply to see her joy. She covered his mouth once more, taking his laughter for her own.

He slipped her shirt from her shoulders, unfastened her bra, pushing the straps along her arms, freeing her breasts. He looked down at her, his eyes dark with pleasure and all of her was freed. She reached for him, bringing his head to her offered breast, sighing without shame as his lips closed on a dark, straining bud, sucking gently. The wet tip of his tongue teased, drawing deeper while the pleasure rose in a heat between her thighs, a low coil in the curve of her abdomen. She arched her back as if it were the only natural movement, giving freely, her hands clinging to the ridges of his upper arms. Her moan came full and thick from the deepest recesses of pleasure.

Laughing softly, pleased by her enjoyment, his mouth dipped to tenderly kiss the round gleam of her belly that gave no indication she was with child. She wished the child there was his. The thought stilled her. Feeling her stillness, he looked up at her, his chin lightly resting on the center of her tummy.

"Don't tell me you've changed your mind," he said, smiling but with the same tenderness with which he touched her. She reached for him even as she closed her eyes to stop the tears that threatened. He rose, came to her and she pulled his face down to hers. Her eyes stayed closed as her parted lips slid across the wide, hard angles of his face only recently healed. Finally she opened her eyes, met the midnight-blue of his and smiled.

"It's just that it wasn't like this. Never," she told him again not in a whisper. "Is this how it is then?"

This is how it should be, the answer came within him. All joy, he thought, seeing its reflection in her eyes, feeling it take hold inside him. "Not always," he told her, suddenly fearful of the rare emotion. He clasped her hands in his and, bringing her arms above her head, kissed her long and deep, covering her with the length and width of his body, his thudding heartbeat matching hers.

He rolled away from her only to take off his clothes. Leaning up on an elbow, she watched. When he lay back down, she skimmed her hand over his ribs, his chest, the hollow of his stomach with fascination. She circled the pebbly tips of his dark nipples with her fingertip, then her lips. Her hand ran up, down his torso, moving lower, touching him. Her fingers curled around him, enclosing him, the throb of blood beating throughout him. With a growl, he turned her on her back, unzipped her pants, pushed down her white cotton panties and bending to her, buried himself in her heat and sweetness. Her moans were low and deep as he tasted the slick slight bud of her. Her shudders began slow, her hips rising, her legs quivering. With a sudden jerk of breath, she pressed her head back, her hips lifting, her body writhing as spasms shook her in release. Her hips sank with no more strength. She lay with her eyes closed, breathing heavily, still trembling.

Her eyes still closed, her fingers found him, tangled in his hair, caressed the side of his face. He moved up the length of her again, and she opened her eyes, cupped his face, kissed his lips sweetly, gratefully and let her tears fall, knowing he would understand.

"It wasn't like that before?" he asked against her mouth.

He saw a woman's wisdom in her honest eyes now as her hand wrapped around him hard and her thighs pressed, open to him once more. She guided him to her, hot and liquid, and he entered her body in a moment with no thought of past or future. A moment of calm as if entering the earth, the sweet, fertile ground. It was then he remembered his responsibility.

"Are you protected?" he asked, loathing the intrusion of such mundane matters in a moment such as this but knowing it necessary. He did not want to cause this woman to cry from sorrow or worry or regret—only from joy.

"Yes, yes," she told him.

As she murmured the answer, she spread her thighs wider, resplendent in her power, and his only thought, his last thought before he drove into her and shattered, was that of hers confessed seconds ago— of "It wasn't like this. Never."

CONSCIOUSNESS CAME BACK. Heavy, rasping breaths remained. The echo of their cries mingled in the air. And too late he realized he had been so worried about protecting Lorna from harm, he'd forgotten to safeguard his own vulnerability. He lay beside her, completely fallen.

He could never stay now.

But for this moment, he must bow his head to her and kiss her slowly and sweetly, letting his lips tell her what he'd never have the courage to say aloud.

She welcomed his lips eagerly as he kissed her with the tenderness that was so much a part of him, something he would only deny. Her arms around him tightened as a sense of coming loss filled her. Good God, she missed him already. She held him, desperate for the feel of him, the warmth, the way he made

her feel—so alive, so feminine, powerful, sexy—
things she'd never been, had never imagined being.

He scooped her into his arms and, sitting up, ar-
ranged her on his lap, looked at her with a warm,
soft darkness in his eyes. She sat on his thighs and
rested her head on his chest, her quiet fingers drawing through the soft down there. His arm wrapped
around her soft, bare middle. She would always remember him. She looked down at her loosely parted
thighs, gleaming unevenly white in moonlight, the
round of her middle. Julius placed his palm there as
if he too knew life grew within. She was quietly
happy and deeply sad.

"Ah, you're sorry now?"

Her head came up and she said, "Oh, no. No,"
with such urgent feeling, he smiled at her, amused.
She smiled back and longed for nothing more than
the deep taste of him inside her. She split her thighs
to straddle him. Her damp hands clutched his shoulders as their mouths melted together. Their tongues
mated. She pressed her flesh to his. She gave in completely to desire.

Her hands massaged his shoulders as she pushed
him onto his back and wrapped her legs around him.
She lowered herself over him, guided him inside. She
felt her own warmth, the hard plunge of him sheathed
within the folds of her body. The spiraling sensation
spread from her parted loins as she arched her back

and cupped her own breasts and rose and fell in endless rhythm. She quivered on the edge, her thighs shaking, her muscles straining. His body reared up, deep inside her, his hands cupping the heavy roundness of her buttocks. He thrust harder, deeper, taking her with him over the edge. Relief exploded in red-hot waves coming, coming, until she collapsed on his chest and lay quivering, feeling his own tremble, hearing his quick, thudding heart. He wrapped his arms around her, absently stroked her back. She reached down and pulled up the afghan Aunt Birdy had crocheted. So cocooned, they slept.

IT WAS STILL night when Julius woke. Lorna had slid off his chest and lay curled beside him. His one arm still held her, draped across her middle. He closed his eyes, breathed in once more the soft sweetness of her hair before releasing her. Careful not to disturb her, he eased himself up, leaned back against the headboard and studied the woman sleeping peacefully beside him. With her hair spread across the sheets, her eyes closed and her breaths deep and even, she looked an angel. The thought caused him to smile. An angel determined to drive him crazy.

His head dropped back to the headboard's edge. He stared at the ceiling. He hadn't expected to sleep. He rarely did more than doze after sex. His limbs always resisted, although heavy with physical pleasure. The intimacy, the closeness kept him alert, on edge. He wouldn't sleep, and the women knew he wouldn't stay. He never stayed. Even Lorna had known he would leave.

Yet, he had slept—a deep, peaceful sleep without concern. He looked down at the woman on her side. One smooth, bare shoulder showed where the covers had slipped. He pulled the bedclothes up and covered her. He smiled, thinking of the Lorna he now knew, the one only hinted at beneath her buttoned-up exterior and bold colors. He smoothed a strand of her hair. How would she surprise him next?

It was time to go. He looked to the half-open door. All he had to do was ease off the bed, dress silently and walk through it, away. Easy.

Lorna sighed, shifted in her sleep, turning toward him as if his thoughts had slipped into her dreams. He looked down at her. Not so easy this time. The realization hit him like a blow to the gut. For the first time, he didn't want to leave. The surprise was on him. His gaze went to the night that had always drawn him before. He saw only darkness while here, in a woman's bed, it was warm, comfortable. Home.

Home. He leaned against the headboard. It wobbled from his weight. Home? The promise of land and a night's sweet lay and he was going soft. It was time to go. He slid out of the bed, dressed silently and walked out into the only home where he'd ever belonged—the darkness.

LORNA HADN'T EXPECTED to find Julius there when she woke and she wasn't disappointed. She'd known he wouldn't stay—not for a night, not for a lifetime. He had made no false promises, freeing them both. She sighed deeply and stretched as if feeling her body for the first time. She looked down to her pendulous breasts, the new fullness of her boyish hips. Such a miracle—all of it—the sex, the womb, the creation of a new life. Of course, she'd known a man was needed to create a child, but who would have thought he was necessary for the creation of herself? She smiled as she stretched once more. Still languid, she rose from the bed, loosely wrapped her robe around her. He would soon be here for breakfast. She went to the kitchen to start the coffee before she dressed for her early-morning walk.

When she returned from her walk, he was sitting at the kitchen table, drinking coffee. She hesitated for a breath, taking in his square, wide back, his shoulders slightly stooped. Then she opened the door, crossing the kitchen with no-nonsense steps. She wouldn't be shy nor remorseful nor embarrassed by her own sexuality. She had neither regrets nor shame. Her regret and shame would have been only if she'd denied herself last night's experience. She might have been a man, so pleased she was with last night's pleasure. She lifted her chin and, when Julius turned his head, his gaze finding her, she said, ''You might've started breakfast. Would it have been too much of an effort to crack an egg or two?''

When his slow, easy smile came, answering her, she grinned, too, even though she was losing the good fight.

She went to the refrigerator, busied herself beginning breakfast. ''Any preferences?'' she asked without looking at him.

''You're not going to go and get all 'wifey' on me now, are you?''

She spun and faced his full grin. She arched her brows, perfected her tone of disdain. ''Hardly.''

''Well, as I recall, I was told 'this isn't a diner, Mr. Holt,''' he taunted her with her own words.

She raised her brow another millimeter. ''Is your underwear up your butt, Julius, or is this just your way of wooing me?''

He laughed, and she wanted nothing more than to kiss those full, laughing lips. Before she gave it a second thought, knowing it would stop her, she moved to him, leaned down and, as he lifted his face to her, kissed him full on the mouth. He pulled her to him, settled her on his lap.

''Is this your way of wooing me, Miss Lorna?'' The twinkle was in his eyes, but she knew the tenderness in his voice surprised him as much as her.

She couldn't help putting her palm softly to his face. ''Let's make a deal. You promise not to woo me, and I'll promise not to woo you.''

His expression sobered. "I don't make promises."

Her other hand lifted to cradle his suddenly serious face. "I would be very disappointed if you did." She kissed him lightly once more, slid off his lap and moved to the stove.

She heard the scrape of his chair, his curse of "Damn woman" as he pulled her into his arms and kissed her dizzy.

Chapter Nine

Once the gate had been opened, it couldn't be closed. Lorna was insatiable, like a teenager, the teenager she'd never been. Freed finally from worry over appearances or conventions or emotional entanglements, she loved for sheer pleasure—hers and Julius's. She was a most willing student, and Julius, she couldn't help thinking with a smile, a most skilled teacher. They made love as naturally as the life all around them here on the farm, the world they'd created together. Where all was safe.

Julius didn't mention leaving again nor did she, although they both knew he would go. Lorna told herself it was part of the relationship's appeal—no promises, no commitments, no strings. She herself had sworn to never marry again. Marriage—what was that but one more convention that she now scorned as easily as wearing chartreuse to her husband's funeral. No, she wouldn't marry, but she would love and, she thought with a Cheshire cat's smile, love she did. How much easier it was without expectations, insecurities, anxieties. They'd become as clever as the wildlife, taking as they pleased, mating for no other reason than that it could be done and it was as pleasurable to share your body with another as it was to take a bath or eat ice cream or walk a long mile with legs strong and faintly aching.

For three weeks, neither spoke of Julius's leaving. It would happen, Lorna had no doubt. To wish otherwise would only ruin what they'd created. He had as little need of a wife and another man's child as she had desire for a husband. They had created something good here, as rich and full as the farm becoming alive all around them. Why did it need to be forever? If it had to be forever, it never would have begun. Such greedy humans we are, Lorna would think.

So she took her fill of him for now, all the while memorizing the fall of his shoulders, the wonderful handfuls of his buttocks. She squirreled away his smiles, devilish, mischievous, seductive, the rare one of tenderness. She gathered his laughter within her. She loved everything about him physically and dared not love more. Once in a while, in the weakest moments after sharing the greatest intimacy, still flushed with pleasure and wonder and bathed by his breath and his body, she longed to share with him the miracle taking place within her womb, the child that would become apparent to all anyway. But she knew that wouldn't be fair to him, that it would unbalance the equation of joy with responsibilities and realities and concern. He said he would be leaving. She did not want him to give pause, to go against his own nature out of obligation.

So, if Julius was to go soon, he need never know. There was no reason.

In the meantime, he prepared her for when he would go, teaching her to thin the fruit and stake the branches and seed the fields and make love like a wild thing.

On the Monday of the fourth week, at breakfast, he carried his dishes to the sink and paused as he looked out the window. "Think I'll take a trip over to Laurel this week, find some pickers." He still hadn't looked at her. "Thought we'd begin your tractor driving lessons today, too, so as you stop pestering me all the time."

Finally he'd turned, taking her gaze into his. He would be gone by the week's end, she thought. And even though she placed her palm firmly on her abdomen as if the life there too had been threatened, she hadn't one regret. Not one regret.

After she cleaned up, she found him in the orchard, the soil between his fingers and a concerned expression on his features.

"If we don't get rain within a day, we'll have to irrigate."

She nodded, always the student now. It was warm

and fat that first week of June, the temperatures in the seventies. The rain and wind had been good and the fruit set would be watched and thinned with crossed fingers. The sunny days were necessary for the bee colonies rented from a local keeper and moved in during the night when the bees weren't in flight. But the temperatures had increased to unseasonable highs the past two days and soil that had only a month or so ago had been mud now was gaining the cracked thirsty look of clay.

"Feel it," he instructed her, sifting the earth in his hand. She squatted down next to him, laying her hand flat on the ground to steady herself.

"Ow!" Quick fire seemed to fill her palm. She raised her hand, saw the red round welt in its center.

"Yellow jacket," Julius said as it buzzed away. He took her hand in his, examined the bite. "Been stung before?"

"Not that I remember. I guess I was always careful."

He glanced at her, then blew softly into her palm's center as if he too could feel the heat and the sting there.

"C'mon." He stood and pulled her to her feet. "We'll put a bit of mud on it and you'll be good as new." He led her to the spigot where there was always a small circle of wet earth where the water dripped. He held her hand the whole way.

"It itches," she said.

"The mud will take care of that. It'll draw the poison out as it dries," he said, smoothing a cool layer onto her palm, blowing again to dry it.

She studied his bowed profile, wanted to kiss him, but knew it wasn't allowed. Theirs had never been a relationship of little gestures. Nor were they a couple in the conventional sense, and so, had no right to hand-holding and swift, sweet, stolen kisses. He held her hand now for medical care only. She studied his bowed head. She was in love with him. How he would laugh if he knew. She herself almost released the dry, sardonic laugh that used to come so easily to her. She was in love with him. Like quick kisses and hand-holding, that wasn't allowed either. Still she wouldn't be sad. No regrets, she remembered.

"It still itches," she complained in the bossy voice he had first come to know.

He glanced at her impatiently. "You'll live. C'mon, we've got to get on with your driving lesson." He held her hand all the way to the barn.

She was climbing up into the driver's seat and settling between his legs when the bottoms of her feet began to burn. The mud had dried, but instead of relief, she felt the itching spreading, up her limbs, her chest, everywhere.

"Julius." She turned to look at him. He touched the vee of skin at her neckline. She looked, saw the red welts rising there.

"Get down. Now."

Panic filled her, was in her voice. "What's happening?"

He scooped her into his arms and ran toward the house. "You must be allergic. You're having a reaction. We've got to get you to a doctor fast. Do you have anything for allergies in the house?"

She shook her head.

"How close is the nearest emergency room?" They reached his truck.

"About fifty minutes away."

He settled her in the truck, looked at the hives spreading up her arms. "Doc Tierney's was on Allen off of Main, right?"

She nodded, too scared to speak.

He slammed the door, rounded the truck and jumped into the driver's seat. "Hang on." He peeled out of the driveway, the force jerking Lorna into her seat. The itching and the heat were becoming unbearable, but she was frightened most of all for her baby. "Don't let anything happen." She sent a whispered prayer to God.

Julius glanced at her. She hadn't realized she'd spoken loud enough for him to understand.

"I won't," he said in the first promise he'd ever made her.

She had to tell him she was pregnant in case she lost consciousness. She didn't want any medications that could possibly harm her child. She was set to tell him about the baby when, as if in response, it felt like her throat was closing up.

"My throat," she said with shallow breaths.

He took one look at her and pressed the gas pedal to the floor. Tires squealing, he turned off the road into the first driveway they came to and jumped out of the truck.

"What are you doing?" She tried to stop him but her breaths were tighter, her throat thicker. She slumped back into the seat, leaning her head back to open her air passages, and tried to breathe.

A moment later, he pulled open the truck door. She looked at him, hating the weakness and fear she knew was in her face. Behind him was Janice Fitzgerald whose husband sold insurance and was doing so well, he'd bought Janice her very own kiln for the ceramic gnomes she created and sold at weekend craft fairs.

"An ambulance is on its way," Julius told Lorna.

"Baby," she tried, before her breath ended again and she had to draw deeply once more.

"Shh. For once try not to have the last word," he said, but his face didn't match his teasing tone. Her hair was in its practical braid, but still he brushed his hand across her forehead as if to smooth away escaped tendrils.

"Baby," she tried to say once more, but her breath was so light. She heard the siren becoming stronger and stronger. Then Julius was gone, running to the road to flag down the ambulance, leaving her with Janice who said, "It'll be all right, honey. They're almost here now."

She couldn't breathe. She leaned forward, coughing, choking, so very scared, when something was put against her mouth and a new voice said, "Breathe slowly."

She jerked back.

"It's okay," the man said, pressing the mask to her mouth once more. "It's only oxygen. You're having an allergic reaction, and this will help you breathe until we get to the hospital. That's it. Breathe."

The tightness in her chest lessened. She breathed deeper.

"Do you think you can climb onto the stretcher?" he asked. She saw three other members of the volunteer rescue squad waiting with a long, white, wheeled bed. She nodded. Her breaths were better.

"Good. You're going to be just fine." The emergency medical technician slipped an elastic around her head to hold the mask in place as she slid down onto the stretcher. She lay back and pulled the mask away from her face.

"No, you've got to keep that on," Julius said, coming forward. The EMT nestling the oxygen tank into the side of the bed glanced up, reached to position the mask once more on her mouth. She looked at him.

"I'm five months pregnant."

She looked at Julius. He froze, stared at her, an unreadable expression on his face. They wheeled her away.

Chapter Ten

The nurse had just adjusted the intravenous drip when Lorna heard the Aunties' voices in the hall.

"The nurse said the second door on the right," Eve said.

"It was the seventh door on the right," Birdy insisted.

"When are you going to start wearing hearing aids and make everyone's life easier?" Eve snapped.

"The day you stop lying about your age," Birdy retorted.

"I'm in here," Lorna called in an attempt to end the argument. Still she smiled when she heard Aunt Eve say with a self-righteous sniff, "I told you it was the second door on the right."

Birdy ignored her sister's triumph and swept into Lorna's room. "My darling." She stopped and clasped her hands to her chest. "Look at you."

"Can the cheap dramatics, Birdy," Eve ordered,

moving past the small woman and coming to Lorna's side.

"How are you, dear?" Eve leaned down, kissed Lorna's forehead, smoothed her brow as she looked into her niece's eyes. In her aunt's eyes, the same gray-green color as her own, Lorna saw the worry Eve was trying not to show. Her aunt straightened. Her hand stayed on Lorna's shoulder.

"Yes, how are you, child?" Birdy came to the other side of the bed and clasped Lorna to her breast. Lorna felt the quick thud of the old woman's heart. She had never meant to frighten these two women.

"Let the child breathe, Bernadette."

"Dotty ol' nag," Aunt Birdy whispered in Lorna's ear before releasing her. She sent Eve a dirty look. Her expression softened as she studied Lorna. She took Lorna's hand in her own.

Lorna smiled, happy they were there—these strong, bossy, quarrelsome women who'd raised her. "I'm okay." She rested her hand on her stomach. "They had to give me adrenaline and antihistamines to bring the reaction under control, but the doctor assured me both medications had been proved safe for pregnant women and their unborn children in the treatment of severe allergies."

Eve crossed herself in a sign of silent thanks. Not to be outdone, Birdy crossed herself, too.

It was then Lorna saw Julius lingering outside the

doorway. She held his gaze a long moment. "I didn't know you were there."

Birdy and Eve looked to the door.

"He called us." Birdy beamed at him. "Thank the Lord we were home."

"What are you hiding back there for?" Eve told him. "Come in, come in."

"Oh yes, come in," Birdy chimed.

Julius raised his palm, declining.

"We're certainly not going to let you stand out in the hall after you saved our niece's life." Birdy went to the door and, hooking her arm through Julius's, dragged him into the room.

"Better do as she says," Eve advised. "She's tiny but stubborn as a mule and twice as ornery."

"It's in the genes," Birdy snapped, the tiny woman pulling Julius into the room as though she'd just caught the legendary ten-pound trout of Laurel River that the men in Hope swore always got away.

"Our hero," Eve noted. Her voice was dry but her face pleased as Birdy dragged Julius to Lorna's side.

My goodness, he was blushing. Lorna smiled at him in sympathy. "Hi, hero."

He shook his head. She saw his gaze flicker to her sheet-covered middle where her hand instinctively rested.

"When I think about what could have happened..." Birdy gave a shudder. "Oh, I just can't even think about it."

"I'm fine, Aunt Birdy." She squeezed the woman's hand. She looked at Aunt Eve. "Really."

"Thanks to this man here," Eve pointed out. "What if you'd been by yourself? Nobody might have known until the crows began to circle."

"Good Lord, Eve, must you be so graphic?"

"Somebody's got to talk some sense into her. You should come home, Lorna May. Where we can take care of you."

"I'm doing just fine taking care of myself."

Eve snorted. "Looks like it."

"I'll be there." Julius spoke for the first time.

Lorna met his impenetrable blue eyes. She shook her head, trying to tell him, no, this wasn't what she wanted. She didn't want him to feel obligated. Trapped. It wasn't his responsibility.

His face was expressionless. "They said you have to stay several more hours."

She nodded. "They want to make sure I don't have any adverse reactions to the medicine."

He shifted, self-conscious in front of the Aunties.

She smiled at him. "Go. I'm fine. They just want to keep me here a few hours for observation."

He shifted again. "I did promise to deliver the John Deere today."

"We'll take good care of her," Birdy assured him.

Julius nodded. He glanced at Lorna once more, then had turned to go when Birdy caught his arm and

Julius found himself in her warm hug. "Thank you for taking care of our girl. You're a hero."

"A hero," Eve echoed solemnly.

Julius shook his head. The "hooked fish" expression had returned to his face. "No, ma'am."

"Yes, you are." Birdy gave him another squeeze. Eve nodded. Julius glanced helplessly at Lorna.

She smiled. "Don't argue. It's the first time they've agreed on anything in years."

HER FATHER CAME a half hour later, walking into the room without a greeting. He stood at the foot of Lorna's bed.

"The doctors said you're fine."

She nodded, her expression as impassive as his.

"And the child is fine, too."

"Yes," she said. Her voice sounded small.

"Thanks to her hired man," Eve added. "He saved her life."

"This wouldn't have even happened if the girl was home where she belonged." Axel spoke as if Lorna wasn't present.

"I am where I belong," she said, forcing her father's cold eyes back to her.

"Ruin yourself if you must but I'll see nothing happens to that child."

Lorna's voice became equally fierce. "Neither will I."

With a final disgusted look, he turned and left.

Birdy, sitting beside Lorna's bed, patted her hand. "He's just worried about you, dear. That's all."

"Sure." Lorna slumped into the pillows, fighting the tears that threatened. "I can feel the love."

Birdy glanced at her sister.

"He wasn't always like that," Eve said.

"Oh no, you should have seen him with your mother. She could make him laugh," Birdy said.

"And go to the shore on picnics. And how she loved to dance. He'd complain the whole time, but, deep down, I think he liked it, too," Eve added.

Lorna knew the stories. When she was a child, she would make the Aunties sit and tell her tales for hours. Her mother had come from the South, her voice like the sweet maple sap that flowed in the spring, her soft slurs rich and exotic among the New Englanders' nasal tones and long vowels. Lorna hadn't inherited any of her beauty or charms.

"He fell harder than the storm that took down the old elm in the town square in '63," Eve noted.

"When she died—" Birdy looked distant "—it was as if part of him died, too. The best part."

Lorna knew her mother only through these stories and pictures and the balloon border she had stenciled on Lorna's nursery walls. The same border Lorna had painted on her own unborn child's bedroom walls. Her mother had died from complications after giving birth to Lorna. And Lorna knew, every time her father looked at her, he thought of that.

THE AUNTIES BROUGHT her back to the farm around supper time. The kitchen was untouched. Julius hadn't eaten yet. She readied a simple meal of soup and sandwiches and waited for his arrival, rehearsing what she would say to him. Supper hour passed. It was growing dark. Still he didn't come. She heated the soup, ate a little, wandered about the kitchen, then put the soup and sandwiches on a platter and went to the trailer.

He wasn't in the trailer. She found him in the fields, squatting among the rows as if talking to the new, rich life there. He looked up as she approached.

She offered the platter. He shook his head. She stood at the field's edge, holding it, feeling awkward. "I got back a few hours ago."

He bent his head to the young plants. "I saw the Aunties bring you home."

"They stayed a bit."

"I know."

"You didn't come up."

"You had company."

"Coward," she teased, hoping to dispel some of the awkwardness between them.

He glanced at her, then straightened, moved to the next row.

She looked at the trellised tendrils and blossoms of the peas. The smells of the spring thaw were long gone, the earthy odor of peat everywhere. "Later on, I'll have to go back for tests, have the injection series once they determine exactly what types of bees I'm allergic to.'' She was stalling, and they both knew it. She was the coward now.

Julius moved to the next row. He stepped lightly as if never more aware of his bulk than among these fragile newborns.

She broke the silence. "I should have told you,"

He looked over at her.

"There were times I wanted to."

"You don't owe me anything.'' He squatted down again.

She stood, watching him. "I owe you, Julius.''

His head swung up, his eyes meeting hers. He shook his head, returned his attention to the ground.

"I didn't tell you about the pregnancy, because I was afraid if you knew, you'd stay not because you wanted to but because you'd feel obligated to.''

He looked up at her. "Lady, you don't know me at all.''

She studied him a second. "Yes, I do.''

He shook his head. "I'm no hero.''

"That's not what the Aunties say.'' She smiled.

His expression stayed serious. "I'm no hero.''

Her face was somber again. "Yes, you are, Julius Holt. But I don't need a hero. And I don't need a husband. And I certainly don't need you to stick around because you feel obligated or sorry for me. That's why I didn't tell you about the baby. Because this baby is my responsibility, and I'm going to take care of it. And not one more person is going to tell me I can't. I can.'' She stomped her foot. ''I can.''

He stared at her, his grin slowly coming.

''Don't you dare smile at me,'' she warned. ''Don't you dare.''

His smile broadened. ''Stomp your foot again. I liked that. It was a nice touch.''

She glared at him. ''You're not obligated to stay. I thank you for all your services.''

His eyebrows wiggled. ''My pleasure, Miss Lorna.''

''I'll prorate your wages for the week and write you a check so you can be gone in the morning.''

''I'm not going anywhere.''

She sighed. ''I told you I don't need a hero.''

''And I told you I'm not a hero.''

''You said you wanted to leave.''

''Did I?''

''Yes.''

''As I recall, you were the one who said I should leave.''

''I didn't want to see anything else happen to you.''

He smiled. ''You like me, don't you?''

''This isn't funny.''

''No, it's not, Miss Lorna.'' He straightened, looked at her sternly. ''I trusted you.''

''What are you talking about?''

''You really expect me to believe leaving here is

for my own good? That your father's put a bounty on my head, and there are some crazy country boys determined to collect it?''

"You don't know him."

"I think it's you I don't know. Or did you think I'd forget?"

"What are you talking about?"

"We had a deal, lady, remember? After the first harvest—profits or land. Convenient, just when the farm is beginning to flourish, you suggest I move on."

"Send me your new address and I'll forward you a check."

He looked around. "You can't send land. Money or land, Miss Lorna. That was the deal."

"You don't want the land, Julius."

"I believe I'll be the one making that decision come November. In the meantime, I'll be sticking around to protect my investment."

She glared at him, her hands on her hips.

"You're not going to stomp your foot, are you?"

"I don't need 'no' charity," she challenged him.

He smiled slow. "I don't need *any* charity. And yes you do. I don't know anyone who couldn't stand a little charity now and then, but that's not what this is." Her own words came back to her.

"You owe me a bonus—land or profits—and I aim to collect."

She lifted her chin. "You don't fool me one bit.

You're hanging around here until the baby comes because you feel obligated.''

He shook his head. "You really think I'd choose to put up with some cranky pregnant widow and her fantasies about being a farmer if there wasn't something in it for me?''

"Yes, I do."

"Lady, you are loony."

"Maybe so, but that doesn't mean I'm not right about you." She looked at him over her shoulder before she left. "Julius, just don't get any notions about falling in love with me now, because I don't want a husband." She flounced away from the field.

"Crazy woman," he yelled after her. She smiled all the way back to the house.

THE DAYS CONTINUED, long and many, the sheer physical demands of the work overriding any other concerns such as emotion. Julius found two fourteen-year-olds anxious to make "real money" and rebellious enough to work for the "ex-con and the crazy widow" as people had come to call these two unlikely partners. The boys were strong as the white pines, their muscles so new they seemed to gleam as the boys would strip to their jeans in a proud peacock display of developing manhood. Julius, who proved to be a gentle taskmaster, would only smile when the boys weren't looking, amused by their strut and grateful for their strength. He taught them, along with

Lorna, many things—some that could be learned by simply looking straight at them—how to stake the long rows of tomatoes and recognize the lettuce—romaine and Boston and red leaf. Other lessons, passed on through Julius from experienced and wiser men, were such as not to work the bean field when it was wet or rust would come into the crop. The Aunties started coming every day, too, Eve with her new acceptance of Julius and her strong will obviously inherited by her niece; Birdy with her hands in flight and her sunny smiles often cast at Julius. After showing Lorna what they'd brought for the baby—never did they come without something to add to the growing supplies for the child—the women donned wide-brimmed hats and marched out into the long rows beneath the high sun, their constant quarreling enough to keep the crows away as they felt along a pod for the certain curve of a ripe pea.

All the while, the land taught Julius. With the work's repetitive and deliberate pace, perseverance and patience was built into every day. The earth, ancient and forever, brought peace.

June moved into July. Julius went to Laurel and found two men who spoke hardly any English but who brought Julius to their priest, who vouched they were good men who came to church every Sunday. They worked beside the boys and the Aunties and Julius, needing no lessons, having worked the fields all their lives—outside of San Juan, then Texas, Florida, New Jersey. Their Spanish floated melodious and distinct in the fields, causing even the Aunties to pause their quarreling and listen. The tractor sounded daily. The rain was little and the irrigation pipe rotated as each day came clear and hot. Yet, despite the constant activity, the full flourish and Lorna's swelling figure, the summer seemed quiet, still, as if it too, like the land, like the land's mistress, was in a state of anticipation.

Lorna moved like a madonna through the fields, bringing jugs of water to fill the cooler and fresh, sugared berries. Still the men and boys were shy around the land's mistress, as well as the sharp-tongued Aunties. The workers brought their own lunches, but Lorna insisted they eat inside in the kitchen, away from the fields for twenty minutes and where she always had extra food. She brought out folding chairs and would sit in the midst of their circle, her hands folded on her swollen belly as if she knew it was the baby that'd brought this most unlikely group together. She'd smile and say, "Look at me. I could barely squat to gather the berries this morning. Soon I'll not be good for anything," and pat her belly proudly. By August, she'd been banished to the stand full-time, which did a brisk business between the housing developments and the closing of the corner markets in the city and those just plum curious about the goings-on out at the old orchard.

It was high summer, and the air didn't move as Julius headed for the house one evening. Sometimes the Aunties joined them but usually, at night, it was just Lorna and him. They ate late, when the sun had dropped and the kitchen wasn't flooded with heat. For two weeks after Lorna's trip to the hospital, they'd kept separate beds. Then one evening, while the katydids sang and a comforting weariness had come to Julius with his full stomach, Lorna pushed back from the table to clear it then stopped and stared at him.

"Did you like having sex with me?"

"Lorna!"

She sat down, totally unperturbed. "I liked having sex with you. Did you like having sex with me?"

He knew she would hound him until he answered. "Yes." He got up from the table to leave.

"So why aren't we sleeping together anymore?"

He studied her, such a fair match. "Because you'll fall in love with me."

She smiled, remembering the taunt first from her lips. "I see no reason why two people who enjoy each other, shouldn't."

"That's your hormones talking. You're in the randy stage of pregnancy."

She laughed. "It beats the 'morning sickness' stage, I'll tell you that."

"Well, it'll pass, too. Just hang in there."

Her gray-green eyes grew solemn. He had turned

to escape before his weak flesh overruled his better judgment when he felt her staying hand on his back.

"I waited my whole life to feel the way you make me feel, Julius."

He looked at her over his shoulder. Her fingertips traced the line of his spine, the jut of his shoulder blade. She'd tilted her face to him, her eyes sincere and too vulnerable. "Why would you make me wait a second more?"

"Damn, Lorna," he cursed, before he grabbed her shoulders, pulled her toward him and kissed her with two weeks of wanting. A long, hard deep kiss that even made him stagger. And he knew he wouldn't ever tell her no again.

SOMETIMES, she would come to him in the evening light; most times, he didn't leave after the night meal was finished but would clear the table, dry the dishes beside her while she washed and chattered and, when all was wiped clean, still beside her, they would go to the spare pale room upstairs that Lorna swore she was painting as soon as she finished the baby's room. But never did he spend the whole night to wake beside her at a farmer's ungodly hour. She also would creep out of his narrow bed, gather her clothes and leave. Neither would stay. They knew better.

He climbed the steps to the back door, saw her through the window bent over the opened oven door. She straightened as he came in and threw him a har-

ried look. Her forehead was damp and her hair curled
at the nape of her neck beneath its loose, twisted
bulk. The kitchen smelled of burnt sugar. She
slammed the oven door closed.

She turned to him as he came in. He sniffed the
hot, heavy air and looked at her expectantly. She
waved away his questions, sighing as she brushed her
damp forehead. She went to the sink and rattled the
soaking dishes. "I made a pie."

He saw the vapors coming from behind the oven
door. He walked over and opened it, waving away
the burning cloud that came from within. He grabbed
a pot holder and pulled out what was supposed to be
a pie. The filling had seeped over the sides and
spilled onto the oven floor. The crust was crisp on
the edges and patched in so many places, it was no
longer respectable. He glanced at Lorna's stiff back.
"I think it's done," he said dubiously.

She turned, marched to the stove, snatched the pot
holder he still held in his hand and picked up the pie.
Carrying it a full arm's length away from her, she
marched out the back door, across the yard to the
trash can by the shed and dumped the pie, plate and
even the pot holder all inside. She slammed the cover
down, brushed off her hands and took a resolute
breath. From the doorway, Julius watched her march
back toward the house. "Uh-oh," he muttered.
"Large enemy aircraft approaching. Major hormonal
attack underway."

She stormed back into the kitchen and stood, hands on hips, glowering at him as if daring him to say something.

"I'll bet it didn't taste bad."

She glared at him a second more. Then he saw her lower lip tremble. *Uh-oh, meltdown in progress.*

She sank onto the closest kitchen chair and dropped her head onto her folded arms on the table.

"Lorna?" he said, as if afraid to ask.

"What?" It was a wail.

"It's nothing to get upset over."

"I'm not upset," she snapped, her head still on her forearms.

"Okay then." He looked helplessly at her slumped figure. "As long as you're not upset."

Chapter Eleven

He stood at a loss for another two seconds, then pulled a chair over beside her and sat. He put his hand carefully on her shoulder. When she didn't shake it off, he moved to her neck, massaged her nape. She lifted her head and looked at him pitifully with red-rimmed eyes.

"Aw, Lorna, come here." He started to gather her onto his lap.

"No, I'm too big."

He scooped her up as if she were a feather and settled her across his thighs. "You're just right."

She wouldn't look into his eyes. "I'm big as a house."

He smoothed the loose hair from her forehead and rubbed her back. "You're pregnant. Pregnant and beautiful."

She looked at him, her eyes grateful as they filled once more. "I'm sorry."

"Sorry? For what? Crying? That's no crime." He

snuggled her against his chest. "You let loose and have yourself a good cry. You're long overdue."

She should have known he'd be kind. She didn't want to cry in front of him. She didn't like to cry in front of anyone. He eased her head down onto his shoulder. His tenderness undid her. She pressed her face to his broad chest and cried her heart out. He sat through it, waiting, rocking her a little, rubbing her back and humming a low tune. Finally she quieted, the storm reduced to no more than annoying hiccups.

He stroked her arm. "Feel better?"

She straightened and tried to swallow a hiccup but it only came out louder. Her nose was probably red, her eyes swollen. "No."

He smiled, rubbed her back.

"I hate crying."

"C'mon, cranky." He rose with her still in his arms.

"Put me down." His strength made her feel weightless, no more than a delicate slip of a woman, she with her size-ten feet and ever-expanding waistline. His power made her feel safe. Loved. All dangerous feelings. "Put me down."

"Hush." He ignored her as he carried her upstairs into the bedroom and laid her on the bed. He slipped off her flat sandals, massaged her puffy ankles. She'd never imagined a man so big whose touch was so delicate.

"Thank you, but you don't have to do that," she told him, still embarrassed by her outburst.

He looked up at her from the foot of the bed. "Stop being so bossy." He smiled his slow grin.

She sank into the pillows propped against the headboard, so very tired. "I think we've entered a new stage of pregnancy." She used the "we" pronoun naturally, becoming aware of its implications after she said it. She could see only his crown past the mound of her stomach, but she could feel his strong, sure hands massaging her feet, her ankles, her calves. She heard his low, throaty laughter.

"You're most definitely right about that," he said.

She closed her eyes. She wanted to remember his laughter, the way it came from deep within his chest and rolled in wave upon wave, seeming to warm everything around him. The laughter that had made her want to laugh, too. When he left, he would take that laughter. She needed to make a memory.

His hands felt so good. She would miss him when he went. She wanted to put her hand gently on his head's dark curls. She rested her hand on her stomach instead. Beneath her palm, a kick fluttered.

"Oh, my God."

"What?" Julius raised his head, concern in his eyes. "What's wrong?"

She shook her head, smiling, overwhelmed. She'd felt flutters before, but it was hard to tell if it was the baby or gas bubbles. This time there was no question. Tears filled her eyes again. She didn't even try to stop them.

"What is it?"

"Give me your hand."

His expression wary, he did as she said.

"Here." She flattened his palm where hers had just rested, covered his hand with her own.

"What?" He was nervous. He stared at their hands.

"Wait," she said softly, trying to calm him.

The baby kicked.

He looked at her, his expression speaking for him. Both her hands lay on his.

"Isn't it amazing? Have you ever felt anything like that in your life?"

Another sharp thrust fed his palm. He pulled his hand away.

"Whoa." Laughing, Lorna covered the spot his hands had warmed. "Scrappy."

"Tough guy," Julius noted.

"Or girl." She smiled at him. He was rubbing his thumb across his palm, the palm that had just felt life.

"A chip off the old block."

"Oh, right." Lorna brushed at the tears still moist on her cheeks. "I'm a veritable Rock of Gibraltar."

Another kick came, causing her to exclaim again, then throw her head back and laugh. When had she become so beautiful? Julius wondered. He stood.

"Okay, little one—" Lorna patted her stomach "—you've made your point. Ow!" She looked up at Julius. "He kicked me again."

"Stubborn and scrappy. You two will get along fine."

She looked at him. She didn't want him to go. Not now. Not ever. The realization was as surprising as the sudden pokes in her womb. Yet she could never ask him to stay. It was an unwritten rule that had allowed their relationship in the first place and would also end it when the time came.

"I'm glad you were here."

He nodded but said nothing. She pushed herself up, swung her legs over the side of the bed.

"What are you doing?" he asked.

"I'm getting up to make supper."

"Lay back down. I'll go get us a pizza."

She shook her head. "I feel fine now. I can make supper." She smiled sheepishly. "Just not dessert."

"Pepperoni or sausage?" was his answer as he walked to the door.

"Oh, okay." She sank back into the bed, surrendering. "Surprise me."

"I'll be back in about forty-five minutes."

She watched him go. One day it would be forever. She remembered the warm heat of his hand on her stomach, the wonderful strong movement of her child. She closed her eyes, made another memory.

HOPE HAD TWO PIZZA PLACES. Julius pulled into a parking place at the first one he came to and went inside. There was a long bar, several tables with red vinyl tablecloths and the smell of Italian cooking.

He walked to the bar and nodded to the men studying him several seats down. A heavyset fellow behind the bar came over to take his order.

"Give me a large pie to go, half pepperoni, half sausage, extra cheese."

"Be about twenty minutes," the man said, writing down the order.

"I'll wait. Give me a draft."

When the beer came, Julius took a sip, keeping his eyes straight ahead, ignoring the other men who still studied him. He thought about Lorna, the life inside her. He could still feel the miracle of movement within her. He had the feeling he would never forget it.

He took another quick sip. Three more months at the most, he told himself. The harvest would be done. The baby would come. He would leave. As he'd always left. Not yet, but soon. Soon.

He waited for the satisfaction the thought of his freedom always gave him. All that came was the thought of Lorna, the farm, the child.

He'd been here too long, that's all. Longest he'd been anywhere in a while. Working the land as if it were his own, eating every night with Lorna as if they were man and wife, watching her grow with the child.

It wasn't even his baby, damn it! It was another man's child. But it also was part of Lorna. And she had become part of him.

He pushed the thought away. He was going soft. The sooner he left, the better. Of that, he had no doubt. He took another sip of beer, waited once more for the thought of his inevitable departure to bring him comfort.

A ramshackle farm and a widow pregnant with her cheating late husband's child. That's what was giving him pause, causing him to wonder about his footloose life? He shook his head and did what he'd taught himself to do years ago when it was the only thing he had left. He laughed.

"Something funny?" The question had no friendliness. Julius looked in the direction it came from, met the surly face of the man seated nearby. He looked familiar. Certainly the challenge in his eyes and the contempt in his face Julius had seen before.

He turned his head, ignoring the man. He'd learned young few fights were worth anything but trouble.

"I asked you a question."

Julius heard the threat in the man's voice. How many times had he heard that tone? Seemed like his whole adult life. Except on the farm where he was treated like a man, not a murderer. That's what was causing all these crazy thoughts to go through his head. It had nothing to do with any other emotion but feeling secure. Secure and soft.

He looked at the man, the other men surrounding him, sharing the same sullen expression.

"What do you want with me?"

"We don't want nothing with you."

He looked straight ahead again, telling himself once more this was a battle he'd never win.

"There isn't a respectable person in this town who wants anything to do with the likes of you."

It was the implied insult to Lorna that sparked Julius's anger.

"We don't want you here, Holt. Understand?"

Julius took a long sip of his beer. "Last I heard, this is a free country."

"Not for killers."

The word hurt. Living with Lorna had made his hard heart feel again. He turned and eyed the man.

The heavyset man who had taken Julius's order had come out of the kitchen and heard the last comment to Julius. "Hey, take it outside," he told the men. "I won't have no trouble in my place."

"There's not going to be any trouble, Lou," the man at the bar said, his gaze staying on Julius. "I was just explaining to Holt here that just because Lorna McDonough is so hard up and crazy as they come, she'll give a bed to a—"

Julius flew off the bar stool and slammed his fist

into the man's face with one smooth motion. The man fell backward onto the floor.

"Hey, that's it," the owner yelled, but the two other men sitting at the bar were already on their feet, fists swinging. The man on the floor got up, came from behind, caught Julius's arms. He broke free, turned to take the man down, no more thought anymore. Only fists and flesh and the taste of blood.

He had just landed a left to the man's face when he heard the sirens. Still he didn't stop, only continued pummeling, the unacknowledged rage of too many wrongs opened like Pandora's box.

"All right. Break it up before I haul all of you yahoos into jail."

It was the word *jail* that made him freeze. Breathing hard, he wiped at his mouth with the back of his hand. A punch caught him in the back, another in the midsection, knocking the air out of him.

"I said that's enough, Sam." A police officer moved into the middle of the group. "Don't think I won't drag you down to county. And I know for a fact Carol won't be too pleased to have to use her cookie jar money to bail your sorry butt out."

Sam looked scornfully at Julius. "He started it."

"That so?" The officer folded his arms, eyeing Julius. "Trouble seems to take a liking to you, boy."

Julius glared at the officer.

"What went on here?" the policeman asked the

owner. He unfolded his arms, rested his hand on the nightstick hanging at his side.

"I told you," Sam interrupted. "He hit me."

"I'm asking Lou here." The policeman addressed the owner. "Is that so?"

Lou looked at Julius. "He threw the first punch."

The officer turned to Julius. "Anything you'd like to add to the story, slick?" Julius silently stared at him, then he swung his head and spit at the man called Sam. The nightstick cracked across the back of his neck, bringing him to his knees. His arms were wrenched behind his back and the cuffs put on. He focused on his anger to fight back the panic of having his freedom taken.

"All right, let's go, killer." The policeman hoisted him up. "And no more funny business or I'm going to stop being Mr. Nice Guy. I'll need you all to come down to the station to sign a statement," he said over his shoulder to the others as he dragged Julius out.

LORNA GLANCED OUT the window for what seemed the hundredth time. All she saw was the land, the darkening night. When Julius left for good, she wondered how long it'd take her before she'd break the habit of looking out the window, waiting to see if he was really gone. He should've been back an hour ago. She waited twenty more minutes, then began to call the pizza places.

JULIUS DIDN'T DEMAND his phone call. There was no one he wanted to call. Even as the door slammed and the bars drew closer and his breathing quickened to shallow, he knew he'd rather spend the night here than let Lorna see him like this—caged, a man no longer but a prisoner. He stood in the cell, looked out the one, small barred window, saw the night falling, knew it fell on the farm, too, and held on to that thought.

He heard heavy steps in the hall but didn't turn away from the window. The steps stopped.

"Here he is," said the detention officer. "You've got a visitor, Holt."

Julius turned to the bars. Axel McDonough stood on the other side.

Axel nodded to the officer.

"He's all yours." The officer walked away.

Julius turned back to the window, the endless sky.

"What do you want with my daughter?"

Julius glanced over his shoulder. The other man's face revealed nothing. Did he love his daughter? Is that why he was here, Julius wondered, or was it he couldn't stand his authority challenged? Julius searched the man's face. Maybe it was a mixture of both? The face remained stone.

"I work her farm."

"Bringing home minimum wage?"

"I don't have a home, McDonough." He wouldn't call him "Boss."

"I'll pay the bail and make it worthwhile for you to be on your way then."

He looked at the man who epitomized everything he'd come to loathe in men of power. "What gave you the impression I was thinking of leaving Hope? Why, I've only begun to enjoy the town's hospitality."

"Don't be a hero, Holt."

Julius's laugh was meant to antagonize. "I'm no hero, McDonough."

"Then you're a fool."

Julius felt the anger rise. Anger that could make a man crazy, lose control. He didn't know who was luckier there were bars between them—Lorna's father or himself. All he knew was he'd begun to care, care too much, a man who had vowed never to care again.

"Name your price, Holt."

"Get out of here."

Axel McDonough's expression never exposed what was behind the cold mask. He turned and walked out.

Julius was left in the silent cell. He could smell the sweat and fear of other men who'd come before him. He didn't know how much time had passed when he heard voices once more. Lorna's voice.

"A person can't go out for a pizza in this town without being put in jail, Frank? Is that what you're telling me?" Her voice was as strong as the August sun, and he could picture her, tall as the men surrounding her, proud in her pregnancy, righteous in her wrath.

"He assaulted Sam Thomas."

"And I'll just bet Sam was sitting there on that bar stool, thinking about last Sunday's sermon when all this began?"

"Witnesses say your man threw the first punch."

"I hope he threw the last one, too. Three on one. At least you boys gave him better odds this time than a few months ago. What? You all warming up to him, Frank?"

"Nobody wants his kind in Hope, Lorna."

"Let me tell you something, Frank Phillips, and at the diner or over at Monk's you can quote me again and again. I've worked side by side with Julius Holt for six months now, and he's a good, hard-working man."

"Well, Lorna, if I remember right, your judgment of character hasn't always been exactly correct."

Oh Lorna, I'm sorry. Julius held fast to the cell's bars.

"Take me to him." Her voice had taken on the natural authority of her father's. Julius let go of the bars, moved back from the door. He stood in the center of the cell, watching her come down the hall. Her face was inscrutable as her father's had been. Julius's was equally impassive. She said nothing as the officer unlocked the door.

"You can pick up your personal belongings at the front desk," he said.

Julius kept his eyes trained on Lorna as he moved toward the open door. She turned her stiff back to him and marched back down the hall. He followed.

She didn't speak, nor did he, as she drove him to where his truck was still parked outside the pizza place. He followed her home. She waited for him in the driveway.

"Come in. Those cuts need cleaning. I don't suppose they fed you, either." She tsked in disgust as she spun and started toward the back of the house, still ready to do battle.

"I don't need you to defend me."

She stopped, spun back to him standing in the driveway. Warrior woman, he thought.

"I can fight my own fights."

She put her hands on her hips, leaned back slightly to adjust the weight of her waistline. "Yeah, you're doing a fine job of it."

She walked toward him, fire in her eyes. "And you just had to fight, right? You let them sucker you right in. You couldn't just sit there and ignore those boobs when they started with their talk. 'Cause talk is talk, that's all it is, sounds in the air that don't exist but for a second."

She took two more steps toward him, her eyes blazing, riled up now. "No, you couldn't just sit there and sip your beer. You had to fight. Why? Why did you have to fight? What was so worth it that you had to fight?''

You. Julius looked into her eyes gone all green with anger and indignation and exasperation, her color high and bright, the strong stance of her body bearing life. *You were worth it.*

She blew out a sigh, waved her hand at him, telling him no answer would suffice anyhow. She stomped off to the back door, furious at him, at herself, at the whole world. She had stepped into that jail, seen him in that cell. And, for a heartbeat, she'd seen the boy, not much more than a child, once locked up like an animal, alone, scared, his world no more than a barred square. All because he'd loved someone and hadn't been able to save her.

She marched into the kitchen, slammed her fist against the nearest wall, reduced to the physical passion she had just denounced. ''Damn him,'' she muttered. ''Damn them.''

She heard the door open. She couldn't turn to face him. Not yet. ''You should leave town.''

''Is that what you want?'' He spoke so quietly. She thought of his tenderness.

''It doesn't matter what I want.''

''Yes, it does,'' he said in that same soft voice.

She turned and faced him, feeling heavy and sad, saw anew his cuts. ''Look at you.''

He smiled. ''Sam and his buddies look worse.''

She shook her head. "I don't know if they'll let you be."

"I've been promised a bonus. I aim to stick around until I can collect it."

She stared at this man as stubborn as she. She shook her head, went to the narrow cupboard where the first aid supplies were shelved. "As long as you're not doing it on my account."

"Did you promise me a bonus or not?"

She brought the bottle of antiseptic and a box of cotton balls to the table. "Sit down, Rocky, and we'll clean you up again."

He sat. She looked at him a moment. He glanced at her expectantly. She leaned forward to inspect his face, involuntarily wincing. She moistened a cotton ball.

"Hey." He put his hand on hers as she dabbed where the skin had split beneath his chin. She met his dark blue eyes. "Thanks."

She turned away, afraid her face was too full of feeling. She took a breath, bent forward, kissed the edge of his jaw, then once more tended his wounds.

Chapter Twelve

Picking began mid-August with the summer apples, but it wasn't until September when the Macs and Cortlands were ready to drop that the real harvest began. The boys returned to school, but Lorna's cash, supplemented with the summer crops and the sale of the John Deere, allowed three more men to be brought in from Laurel. The Aunties also came every day to bag and police the "pick-your-own" and argue and comment on the others. Eight to nine hours a day, one apple at a time like the single step of a journey was twisted off the tree and set carefully in the kidney-shaped buckets with the canvas bottoms. The orchard was littered with ladders and pickers and buckets. The boxes, weathered the gray of apple-tree bark itself, filled until Lorna no long read with foreboding the names on their sides—Loveland, Harvest Hill, Lakeside—all orchards abandoned or lost to industry.

The season was a week old when the weather

channel warned of a fast-moving warm front coming up the coast, which could cause severe storms. "Surely, it'll blow out to sea before it gets here," Lorna said in her strongest voice, watching Julius as he listened to the report.

He stood his face solemn. "We'll pick as much as possible today." She got up, too, followed him as he walked to the door. He stopped.

"Where are you going?"

"To pick." She tried to move past him.

He blocked her way. "No."

She raised her eyebrows. "No?"

He looked down at her large belly. "Pregnant ladies don't pick."

"Horsefeathers."

"Horsefeathers?" Here came that slow, infuriatingly sexy grin.

"Move out of my way, big man, or I'll say much worse."

"You're eight months pregnant, remember?"

She put her hands on her hips. "And healthy and strong as a horse."

"And stubborn as a goat."

They stood for a silent second, squared off.

She looked at him in appeal. "This is my orchard. Please let me help." She saw the softening in his eyes and knew she was winning. "Only for one day—until the storm threat passes. I would do nothing to harm this baby. You know that."

He sighed with such exasperation she knew she'd won.

"No climbing."

"What?" she exclaimed as she followed him outside. "Do you think I'm crazy?"

"Without a doubt." They headed to the orchard.

The Aunties insisted on picking, too, when they came, much to the men's consternation, but, with the same stubborn streak inherited by their niece, they slung the straps of the apple buckets low across their shoulders, handling the apples like eggs to avoid bruising. Lorna slung her bucket over her shoulder and to the side, letting it rest against the full curve of her waist and emptying its drawstring bottom into the boxes when it was only a third full. The apples gathered, clustered within the boxes smelling of the soil, and, after each deposit, Lorna walked back to the waiting trees with the longest strides possible, as if stepping straight into the future.

Yet all knew, no matter how much was gathered today, if the storm hit, the rest of the crop would be wiped out. Lorna worked steadily but slowly, even resting without complaint when the Aunties insisted. She wore sneakers and her most comfortable outfit—a denim jumper that hung loose about her burgeoning figure. By two, the sky had begun to gray and fill and glances became uneasy. Still, as the Aunties ordered, Lorna sat down on the wicker rocker Julius had carried down from the house, resting her feet on an overturned crate. She sipped from a water bottle, smiled encouragingly at Julius as he hauled another flat to the storage room to be picked up by the packinghouse at the end of the day. She heard the sound of the tractor returning and stood, rested and more than ready to work. She was walking toward her waiting bucket when she heard Aunt Birdy gasp.

"What'd you do? Break another nail, Birdy?" Eve dismissed her sister's frequent theatrics. But it was Eve's "Oh my Lord above" that made Lorna stop. She turned and looked at her aunts. Eve was struggling out of her bucket, the apples falling, rolling.

"What's the matter?" Lorna froze at their expressions.

"Your skirt…" Birdy also hadn't moved.

"Go call 911. Get Julius," Eve ordered her sister.

"What's the matter?" Lorna's voice was as frantic as Birdy's. Eve reached her and touched her backside. "You're bleeding. Don't you feel it?"

Lorna looked behind her, saw the spreading dark stain across the back of her jumper. She looked at Eve. "It felt a little damp when I was sitting, but I thought it was just sweat…" Fear filled her.

"Everything will be fine. The ambulance is on its way. Let's sit you down."

Eve wrapped her arm around Lorna's shoulders, took her elbow and led her back to the rocker. Lorna felt the warmth between her legs now, the very top of her inner thighs. She saw the faint red on the rocker seat. She clutched her aunt's hand. "The baby, the baby."

Julius was crossing the field, running toward her. He gathered her in his arms and carried her out of the orchard.

She clung to his neck, pressed her face into his warm chest, no longer strong at all. "The baby, the baby," she murmured.

"Shh. I've got you. I'm not going to let anything happen to you or this baby."

She felt the strong set to his steps, the firm support of his arms, not unlike the first day he'd come. He'd carried her then. He carried her now. She looked for the medal. The gold relief of Saint Nicholas glinted. She prayed.

Aunt Eve followed right behind them. Aunt Birdy came out the back door, wringing her hands. "The ambulance is on its way."

"Lay her down in the front room," Eve ordered. "She needs to lie down."

Julius carried her into the front room, gently put her on the rarely used couch.

"Thank you." Scared and overwrought with emotion, she grabbed his hand and clung to it, not wanting him to leave her yet. No, she could no longer be strong.

He looked down at her, a rare helplessness in those blue eyes. He looked to the Aunties as his fingers tightened on hers. "I should take her to the emergency room."

"No, she needs to lie down," Eve argued at Lorna's other side.

"The emergency team will be here any moment," Birdy beside her sister reassured. "They've got medical equipment, training, they're professionals." She leaned over the back of the couch, brushed the hair that always hung free now off Lorna's forehead.

"Everything will be okay," Eve insisted.

Julius looked down at Lorna, nodding agreement, even though the haunted look was still in his eyes. She raised his hand, pressed his fingertips to her lips, afraid for the baby, for her, for him, for them all.

He covered her hand in his, held it in his own, leaned down to kiss her forehead. "Everything will be okay."

"I know." She lied, too.

The ambulance siren carried easily across the last long, open acres of land. Eve and Birdy went to the porch to meet them. Julius stayed with Lorna. Neither spoke. Words were useless now.

The front door swung open. The stretcher rolled in. Lorna looked at Julius, finally spoke. "Does your knee say it's going to storm?"

He didn't want to lie to her, yet he couldn't speak. She took his breath away.

She squeezed his hand. "Stay here. Get as much as the crop in as possible."

He nodded, found his voice. "Always the boss," he said softly.

She half smiled, and said just as softly, "Don't you forget it." She squeezed his fingers once more, then he had to step aside. He watched them lift her onto the stretcher, fasten the blood pressure cuff around her upper arm, put the stethoscope to her stomach.

"Good strong heart," the medical technician assured her as they rolled her to the front door.

"Is my baby okay?"

"We'll get you to the hospital and take it from there," the technician answered without answering.

They rolled her across the porch and lifted the stretcher down the stairs. She waited until she saw the sky above, then she closed her eyes and prayed for her baby. She opened her eyes as they slid her into the back of the ambulance. She saw Julius framed by her glorious yellow shutters. The ambulance doors slammed shut. The siren screamed. Even still, just before they reached the hospital, Lorna heard the hard *ping-ping-ping* of precipitation against the vehicle's roof.

JULIUS SAT in the third floor visitors' area and waited. The hailstorm had lasted only twenty-five minutes, bouncing off the roofs, rebounding onto the apples, pummeling the Baldwins, Cortlands, Northern Spies, marking the fruit, shots that would only spread as the apples ripened. There would be seconds, drops, cider, but overall, whatever had been on the branches was ruined. He'd stood with the men from Laurel huddled beneath the barn's back overhang, watching the storm, feeling with each hit as helpless as the hail flung from above.

One of the men had lit an unfiltered cigarette, spit a piece of tobacco from his tongue, inhaled deeply. "Next season," he'd said, watching his smoke curl up into the storm like a sign.

The Aunties came down the hall and found Julius on the falsely cheerful orange vinyl couch, staring at the TV with its sound off. They sat down on either side of him, neither speaking. It was this uncustomary silence that caused him to fear the worst. He looked at one, then the other. His heart prayed.

Birdy patted his hand gripping the edge of the couch. "Our girl's okay." He closed his eyes and, for the first time that he could remember in his life, he rejoiced. But when he opened his eyes and saw the Aunties' expressions still so grave, he realized his joy had been premature.

"The baby?" He'd never heard his voice so fearful.

"The baby's okay…"

Again relief flooded through him. He'd been careful for so long not to care that he'd forgotten some emotions could be so sweet.

"…this time." Eve's lips pressed tight with worry.

"What do you mean?" The sweetness slowly drained from him.

"Lorna was lucky. The bleeding was from a blood clot that she must have developed early on in the pregnancy. Today's physical activity tore it loose from where it had attached to the uterine lining. From what the ultrasounds show, there was no damage. The placenta seems to still be attached. No harm was done to Lorna or the baby...this time," she added again.

Birdy gripped Julius's hand and smiled up at him. "It's a boy."

Emotion, so long without voice within Julius, now would not be silent. He squeezed Birdy's thin-boned hand as feeling flooded him.

"The doctor said there is some slight dilation of the cervix, but that's not unusual at this stage," Eve continued. "He suggested she stay off her feet for a day or two. Definitely no more strenuous activity."

Julius nodded. "I told her this morning she was crazy to pick—"

"She needs to come home, Julius."

He looked at Eve. He didn't know what to say.

"We'll take care of her," Birdy put forth gently.

His eyes went to the silent screen, stared at the picture without seeing it. "You said she's okay."

"This time."

He turned to Eve.

"First, there was the episode with the bee sting, now this. Three times and you're out, Julius."

"We just don't want her to take any more chances." Birdy squeezed Julius's hand.

"She should be in town, closer to the hospital," Eve argued.

He stared straight ahead. "She won't leave the farm."

"It won't be forever," Eve said.

"Only for a little while." Birdy's tone was milder. "Until the baby comes and she's back on her feet again."

He looked at the ladies, shook his head. "She won't leave the farm."

Eve met his gaze. "If you leave, she would."

Julius stared at her wordlessly.

"She'd have to then," Birdy agreed.

"The hailstorm finished the harvest. The pickers will be moving on. The season's over," Eve said.

Julius looked past the older woman. *The season's over.* Time to go.

"Even Lorna wouldn't be foolish enough to stay on the farm all alone, miles from no one, in her current condition," Eve said.

"She was happy there," Julius said quietly. As was he. The season is over. Time to go.

"Lord knows, the farm will still be there, but right now, Lorna doesn't need to worry about money and crops and the wicked weather. She needs to worry about herself and her baby.''

''We can't let anything happen to the baby, Julius,'' Birdy appealed.

''No.'' Eve's voice became even firmer. ''We won't let anything happen to the baby.''

''I could stay.'' The words surprised Julius as much as the women. He'd always left for as long as he could remember. He'd never even considered an alternative.

The Aunties looked at each other. ''For how long?'' Eve asked.

He had no answer. He'd never stayed before.

''And even if you do stay, where would that leave Lorna?''

He looked at Eve, not understanding her sharp words.

''What my sister means,'' Birdy said in a soothing tone, ''is that Lorna is still a young woman. The story of her first ill-fated marriage will probably always provide fodder for entertainment but, one day, the talk will die down, and Lorna's gosh-awful attempts to prove she doesn't give a fig about it all will subside, and she might even find herself wanting to marry, give her child a father and siblings. Family.''

''And even if she doesn't come to her senses and want to marry—'' Eve's tone was matter-of-fact ''—the child will have a tough enough row to hoe with the details of his mother's past. Any other speculation, well…''

Julius understood. He was a man who'd taken another man's life. An ex-con. That's all he'd ever be to others, to himself. After so many times, it shouldn't hurt, but he'd allowed himself to become vulnerable. He'd let himself hope…hope…and this time it hurt the worst of all.

''We'll bring her home,'' Eve assured him. ''She'll have the best possible care until the baby is born, and then, if she wants to, and once she's strong again, she can go back to the farm.''

''What does her father say? Does he want her home, too?''

''Oh, yes, yes.'' Birdy's emphatic answer surprised Julius.

''We know our brother is a hard man,'' Eve said. ''When he lost Lorna's mother, I didn't think he'd survive. He did, but what was left of him became hard and distant and controlling. And he's done some things that were just downright wrong, but I can tell you this, everything—everything—he's done has been to protect Lorna from harm. It's the only thing that scares him. She's all he has left and he's as afraid of that fact as he is that something will happen to her…just like her mother.''

A rare note of plea came into Eve's voice. ''This baby might be the last chance for my brother and his daughter. Give them that chance. If not for them, think of the child.''

Julius looked at the woman's earnest expression.

"Let us bring our girl home, Julius.''

He nodded.

LORNA smiled as he came into the room. She watched him as he came toward her. Her smile grew sad. "You're leaving, aren't you?'' she said softly.

He couldn't speak. How did she know everything about him? Did she know he loved her, a fact he himself had only begun to realize? It was past time for him to go. It was for the best—for her, for him. No more pain.

"We sent on what we got in before the storm to the packing house. We're gathering the seconds, the drops. They'll take those for the cider presses and—''

"Stop sugarcoating it for me. I'm a big girl.'' She patted her middle.

He looked at her stomach rising beneath the thin sheet. "The Aunties said it was a boy.''

Lorna smiled. "They watched the ultrasound with me. For the first hour after, they ran around, telling anyone within earshot that the doctor had showed them 'his perfect little pickle.'''

Julius laughed. He looked at Lorna. His expression sobered. "The hail finished everything. The season's over.''

She looked away to the window, her face somber now, his heart breaking. But when she looked back at him, she smiled a small smile. "There'll be another season," she said, as wise as the old man who'd stood with him today in the storm; speaking as one who knew the fields as intimately as a lover's body and desired them as much.

"Your family wants you home, Lorna."

She stared at him as if he were a traitor. He reached behind his neck, unclasped the gold chain he was never without.

"Saint Nicholas," Lorna murmured. "Patron saint of travelers."

"Children," he whispered, his breath sweet and warm as he leaned down to fasten the chain around her neck.

She touched the gold circle at her throat's hollow. "Old maids."

He shook his head.

She raised her hands to unfasten the necklace. "I can't, Julius—"

"No." He clasped her forearm. "It's the only thing I have of value. It was my sister's."

She stopped, arms mid-motion.

Her arms dropped.

"The doctor said you need to take it easy. No more strenuous activity."

She waved her hand impatiently, dismissing his

concern. "Doctors are always overcautious. I feel terrific, strong."

"You need to let someone take care of you. Someone who loves you."

She looked at him. He wanted to turn away from what he saw in those honest eyes. "I can take care of myself."

"You're stubborn but I know you're not selfish, Lorna. Think of your baby."

She tightened her expression, anger at him in her eyes now.

"Go home. Let them take care of you until the baby comes and you're both strong again...and a new season comes."

The anger in her eyes slowly faded and was replaced by resignation. "You're right, of course." She smiled boldly, bright as the colors she loved, but beneath, he saw bittersweet sadness.

He kissed those sweet, sad lips one last time. Her arms wrapped around his neck. She clung to him for a moment. Then she let him go.

He straightened, brushed her cheek. "You're a helluva woman, Miss Lorna. You remember that." He leaned down, kissed her belly and the child beneath. He straightened, looked at her one last time, prepared to go. He never said goodbye, just left. And so it would be this time.

"The men's paychecks for this week are in the

desk drawer in the front room. I'll write you your bonus before you leave."

He shook his head.

"A deal's a deal, Julius."

"The deal was a percentage of the profits or land. There'll be no profits this year."

"There's land."

He let the smile that'd always saved him in the past come. "What would I do with land?" he asked, denying his love for the farm as easily as his love for her.

He turned to go, but she caught his hand. He turned to her. "I wish," she said, still sweetly, sadly smiling. Her voice broke and she turned her head. He became afraid to hear what she would say. Still she held his hand and he could not let go.

"I wish I hadn't promised myself..." She turned to him, her smile soft and her eyes the colors of an ever-running river. "I wish I hadn't promised myself that I wouldn't ask you to stay."

Chapter Thirteen

Lord, she was miserable. Due to her advanced stage of pregnancy, she'd been required to stay at the hospital overnight for observation but the next morning the Aunties had come bright and early, nagging the nurses and any other personnel that passed in the hall until Lorna was discharged. Once in the car, they turned toward the McDonough home standing sentinel over Hope.

"But my things," Lorna had protested. "I have to go to the farm, get some clothes."

Birdy in the back seat leaned forward to pat her niece's shoulder. "We've already been there, dear. We packed everything you need—clothes, undergarments, vitamins, books—"

"Those horrid overalls that make you look like Junior Walton." Eve rolled her eyes.

"The baby's things, even the—"

"But what about the men, the apples—"

"Everything is all taken care of. What's left will

be picked and sold to the packing house for seconds. Julius will give the men their final checks. He'll make sure everything is done, packed up, shut down.''

"He's still there?'' She hated herself even for asking.

Eve glanced at her sharply. "He'll be leaving as soon as everything's finished and the trucks have picked up what's left. Birdy and I will go out later this week to make sure everything's shipshape.''

Lorna sank into the seat, looked out the window. She missed the farm already. "You know, there's no reason I can't rest in bed just as easily out there. You two could come and stay with me—''

Eve sent her another sharp look. "What would be the sense in that when you have a home right here in town, closer to the hospital should something else happen? You've been lucky twice before, Lorna May, but don't test the fates. If anything happened to that baby boy of yours, we'd never forgive ourselves. And neither would you.''

Lorna sighed. "You're right. I'm just being stubborn.''

Birdy leaned forward, patted her shoulder again. "We wouldn't expect anything less, dear.''

Lorna saw her father's Lincoln as soon as they crested the top of the long driveway. "What's he doing home this time of day? Shouldn't he be at work?''

Eve pulled up to the house's side entrance. "I'll let you off here."

"I can walk from the garage, Aunt Eve." She was nervous.

"Nonsense. Birdy and I will bring in your things. Get out."

"Aunt—"

"No strenuous activity," Eve ordered.

Lorna knew from her aunt's tone, arguing would be a waste of time. She opened the door as told and got out. She stood there a minute, staring up at the huge white house with its classic black shutters. She imagined them the bold, brilliant yellow of the farmhouse. She smiled and felt strong enough to step toward the door. Still she walked slowly, rehearsing what she would say to her father. *This is only temporary,* she would tell him first off. *As soon as the child is born and everything is fine, I'll be going back to the farm.*

She opened the side door and went inside. Two large oaks sheltered the side of the house and the hall was always cool, the house silent. She shut the door behind her and stood in the center of the marble-tiled hall, not quite sure where to go.

She started toward the kitchen, heard movement and turned to meet her father coming out of the dark library to the far right. "This is only—" she began her speech before he could begin his reprimands when she saw an expression of complete wonder wash across his face. He looked at her, seeing her for the first time full with child. Just as quickly the wonder was gone, but before the stern lines returned, a flash of relief lit his eyes.

She folded her hands on her stomach. "The doctor says it's a boy."

He nodded approval, staring at her stomach. "And he's okay?"

"Yes."

His gaze lifted to her face. "And you?"

He spoke matter-of-factly, but she remembered his amazement exposed only seconds ago. "I'm okay."

He nodded again brusquely.

"And you?" she asked.

He dismissed her concern with a quick wave, staring at her as if truly seeing her for the first time. "It's about time that—" He was silent for a second, then said, "It's good you're here."

"It's only—" She hesitated, too. His speech had waited. So could hers. "It's good to be here."

They stood awkwardly. Lorna heard the aunts' bickering voices outside as they approached the house. Her father rolled his eyes.

"I guess I'd better go out there and help before they start throwing my things at each other," Lorna said.

"They brought some of your things last night. I had them put them in the yellow bedroom on the east side instead of your old room."

Lorna turned and looked at her father.

"In the morning, if the sun's strong, it's bright enough in there to hurt your eyes."

Her father had seen her yellow shutters, her blue door. Lorna smiled.

"And there's a smaller connecting room good for a crib and whatnot."

"Thank you." She should have told him this was only temporary, she realized. "I'm grateful..." She didn't want to hurt him, but if she waited, it would be worse. "I'm grateful..."

"Later on, you'll need some place to lay the baby down when you come back for visits, Sunday dinners, holidays, whatever. And you know those ol' biddies aren't going to give you or me a moment's peace if you don't let them take the child overnight once in a while...when you feel he's ready."

Gratitude welled up inside Lorna "Thank you."

Her father waved his hand again. "I'd better get to the salt mine before we all starve."

The side door opened behind them. And the aunts came in, dragging a box between them.

"Good Lord, Bernadette, are you trying to give us both double hernias?" Eve complained.

Lorna turned back to her father to share a smile, but he was already gone.

OVER A WEEK HAD PASSED and Lorna had only grown more restless and frustrated each day, although she was careful not to let her unhappiness show. This was for the best, she kept telling herself. Just as everyone had told her.

She lay on the bed in the bright yellow bedroom. Birdy lay propped beside her, watching her favorite afternoon soap. "Now that one there, she changes partners quicker than a Virginia reel," Birdy said indignantly as she filled Lorna in on all the intrigues and histories.

"What about that one?" Lorna pointed to a male lead. "He's sexy, don't you think?" She wriggled her eyebrows.

"Him?" Aunt Birdy stared at the screen. "Oh no. His wife came home early from work to tell him the news of her pregnancy and found him with Lance's wife in a compromising position."

"She didn't shoot his pickle off, did she?"

"She should have," Birdy declared. Realizing what she'd said, she looked at Lorna. "Oh, honey, I didn't mean—"

Lorna laughed. "Oh, Aunt Birdy, it's all right, really." She chuckled. "You've got to laugh, you know. Life is just so damn funny sometimes, isn't it?"

Birdy studied her niece. "I suppose it is." She turned her attention back to the show. "Now, that one there," she said as an older, distinguished-looking male actor came onto the screen, "he can eat crackers in my bed anytime.'' She winked at her niece.

"Aunt Birdy, you're wicked."

Birdy shrugged. "It passes the time." She watched her show, her smile slowly dissolving, a rare sadness in her expression.

Lorna studied the older woman a few seconds. "Do you still think of him?" she asked. She didn't even have to say his name. Birdy would know she was referring to the man her aunt had been in love with when she was so very young. They were to be married when he returned from the war. He'd never returned.

"My goodness, such questions." Birdy said nothing more, and Lorna thought the subject closed.

"He was such a boy really…just a boy."

Birdy's cheeks had taken on a high color. Softness stole into her eyes as she stared at the television.

"So long ago," she dismissed.

"Do you wish you'd defied your father and mother and married him before he went off to the war instead of promising to wait for him?"

Birdy turned to her niece. "I'll tell you what I do wish." A mischievous twinkle lessened the woman's somber expression. "I wish I'd slept with him before he left."

The two women chuckled. Birdy turned her attention back to the show.

"Did you ever stop loving him?"

Aunt Birdy smiled, but her answer was in the sadness in her eyes. "Such questions." She patted her niece's hand. "What was to be, was."

The two women watched the show in silence for a few minutes.

"Do you think he'll come back, Aunt Birdy?" She spoke of Julius.

Birdy glanced at her niece. From her aunt's concerned expression, Lorna knew her own sadness now showed. She smiled brightly, but her aunt's expression stayed worried.

"You'll be all right, dear."

Lorna nodded, faced the TV. "I just...I just didn't expect to miss him so much."

"Of course, you do."

Lorna slumped back against the headboard. "It's my own fault again. Just like before." She shook her head, smiled ruefully. "'Loony Lorna.'"

"Don't call yourself that, dear."

"Well, I must be crazy. You'd think I'd learn. And the hell of it is I knew all along he was going to leave. Right from the beginning, first thing he told me, right up front. So, I don't know why I'm sitting here asking why he left?"

"That's easy, dear. He left because he loved you."

"Oh no, Aunt Birdy. He didn't love me. If he loved me, he would've stayed."

Watching the show, Birdy said off-handedly, "He would've stayed. For you. He wanted to. Put up a pretty good argument, too, but when Eve explained to him it was best for you and the baby to be here and the only way we'd get you here is if he left you all alone on the farm, he understood.'' She patted her niece's hand. ''Just like you did.'' The show's closing credits began to roll. ''It's over? They're going to leave us hanging like that?''

She got up off the bed. ''I don't know why I torture myself with these things.'' She smiled down at her niece. ''You know what we need. Some of Eve's Pepperidge Farm cookies that she squirrels away. I'll go break into her secret stash. It drives her insane. I'll be right back with the booty.''

''Aunt Birdy?'' Lorna sat, stunned by her aunt's revelations.

The older woman turned at the door.

''Julius wanted to leave.''

Birdy considered her niece. ''You knew him best, dear. All I know is we sure had to talk him into it.''

Lorna dropped back against the pillows. She should have known. She should have fought harder. What had happened to the woman she'd become those past months? For over a week now they'd kept her tethered to this bed like an unruly foal needing to be broken. And she'd let them. One little setback, and she'd changed back into the good little girl that did as she was told.

She placed her hands on the round rise of her middle and felt the fierce strength swell again inside her. "Sorry, kiddo. I won't let you down again."

She only wished she had the same chance to apologize to Julius. She'd been as quick to condemn him as the others, accepting so easily when he said it was better he left, that he was no good for her or her child. She should have argued; she should have told him he was the best thing that'd ever happened to her. She should have told him she loved him. Maybe it wouldn't have made a difference to him, but it would have made a difference to her. She should have fought harder for him. She opened her eyes again to the silly shape of her.

"Well, kiddo—" she patted her stomach "—maybe it's too late for Julius and me, but it's not too late for me and you."

She was packing when Birdy returned with a tray of tea and cookies. "Ha! She switched her hiding place, but I—Lorna, what are you doing out of bed?"

She flashed the woman a bright, saucy smile. "I'm fine, Aunt Birdy."

Birdy set down the tray. "But the doctor said—"

"The doctor said, 'Take it easy. Nothing strenuous for a day or two.' I've been lying around for over a week."

"But Lorna, are you strong enough—"

"Aunt Birdy." Lorna moved to the tiny woman, took her hands in hers. "I'm stronger than I've ever been in my life."

"But the baby?"

"Don't worry. I won't let anything happen to the baby." Lorna kissed and hugged her aunt, then picked up the small overnight bag and moved to the door.

"But where are you going?"

"Home, Aunt Birdy." She was singing. "I'm going home."

SHE FOLLOWED the familiar road, smiling as she rounded the bend, and saw the blinding yellow shutters, the vibrant blue door. She'd been away a little more than a week. It seemed a lifetime. She pulled into the driveway. She looked to the orchard's long rows. "You're still standing, aren't you? Still strong." She saluted the barren trees. "Don't worry. Next year. I'll be here and so will you. Next year."

She walked to the back door and saw the trailer where Julius had slept. She let the pang come but didn't stop moving. God, she would miss him. She unlocked the door, went inside. The sun filled the kitchen as if to welcome her home. She smiled, patted her stomach. "We're back, kiddo. We're home."

She was upstairs in the bedroom, unpacking the small bag she'd brought with her when she heard a vehicle pull into the driveway. "Didn't take long for the cavalry to arrive," she muttered, more amused than annoyed, knowing she was strong enough to let her family love her without sacrificing herself. She heard the back door open, steps crossing the first floor, coming up the stairs. "I'm in the bedroom and I'm still breathing," she called.

"Lorna?"

The deep voice spun her around. She saw the man filling the door frame, the dark blue eyes that always held her. "Julius," she softly murmured as if dreaming. *He didn't leave. He didn't leave.* Joy soared through her, even stronger than her shock.

He stepped into the room, as incredulous as she. "What are you doing here?"

She smiled. "This is where I belong."

He studied her. "I got as far as the county line when I turned around." His voice was still mystified. "I told myself I'd just stay a day or two more, make sure everything was taken care of."

"It's been longer?"

"Four days."

Lorna smiled.

Julius ran his hand through the long length of his hair. He looked to the window. "I told myself it was the land."

She smiled ruefully. "That's about all that's left."

His gaze moved back to her. "It wasn't the land, Lorna."

The sound of her name in his voice trembled through her, spoke to the ache inside her for the past week. *Lord, she'd missed him.*

His expression grew worried. "Shouldn't you be at your father's house?"

She shook her head. "No, this is where I should be, Julius. This is my home." She gathered every ounce of strength she'd gained over the past year, strength she'd given herself; strength Julius had given her. "It's your home, too, Julius, if you want it to be."

He closed his eyes and slowly shook his head. Her heart broke. When he opened his eyes, she saw a tremulous gleam.

"You're my home, Lorna. You're my home."

She moved toward him. Carefully his arms came around her as if afraid she'd shatter. Oh, this gentle, gentle man, afraid as she had been. She touched the face she didn't think she'd ever see again, smiled into the eyes she'd thought were gone forever. He still could leave, the small voice inside her told her, but she was strong enough to take that chance. She wasn't afraid anymore.

"I love you," she told him.

She felt him stiffen, felt his fear. "It's all right," she assured him.

"No." He stepped back, held her lightly by her upper arms. "If I care, begin to care…" He lowered his head, took his hands off her. "I killed a man, Lorna. If I hadn't…" He looked down at his hands. "I saw his breath stop, his…" He looked away, horror in his eyes.

"You were a boy, Julius. Just a boy. You made a mistake. There's been no trouble since then."

"I haven't cared about anything since then." His gaze hardened. "I killed a man. You can't change that."

"You're a good man. A good man. Don't believe otherwise."

"Why? Why do you believe in me?"

She smiled. "That's simple. You believed in me."

He kissed her with the tenderness she never thought of him without. Full and flush with life, she leaned against his hard chest, all the pain of the past few days leaving at the soft touch of his mouth. As if in contrast to this exquisite gentleness, the sensual demand flowing in her took on a fierceness, taking them both to where all was only a powerful wave of need.

Her fingers clenched and unclenched the rough cotton of his shirt as she leaned in to his hard, lean body, seeking everything only he could give her. His mouth became wonderfully heavy on hers until, with a soundless sigh of pleasure, she parted her lips and moaned into his mouth. His tongue came inside her, tasting her, taunting her, taking her deeper into the whirlwind of sensuality.

He wrenched his mouth from hers, dropped his head to her chest, pressing a kiss to the hollow of her throat, breathing heavy. He looked to the wondrous rise of her belly. He ran his hands gently, amazedly, along the full curve of her middle, knelt down and kissed her center, her flattened navel. She bowed her head, curving to him, the need so overwhelming, the emotion so sweet. She lowered herself and, kneeling opposite, caught his rough face in her hands.

"You're a good man, Julius. I wish the child were yours."

He closed his eyes, concealing the emotion there, but beneath the features of a man came the face of a boy, forever alone, fearful, lost. She put her palms to his wide cheekbones. He raised one hand to hers, gripped her fingers, kissed their tips.

He opened his eyes, hooded with pain. "I'm not the man for you, Lorna."

She smiled. "I will have no other."

"Stubborn." He dropped his head, kissed her cheek, her forehead. "Stubborn, stubborn."

"Stay with me." It was a prayer, a plea. "If only for now."

He gathered her to him, pressed his forehead to hers, kissed a corner of her mouth. "You didn't even have to ask."

Together they stood, clinging to each other, the strong forces around them, within them seeking to sweep them away. He claimed her mouth once more, deepening the kiss into sighs of soft desire. She put her arms around him, his muscles so powerful, almost violent beneath her touch. Such weight, such strength, such power within her grasp, she should shrink back with fright. But there was no fear. Not here, not with this man so large, so looming but so infinitely tender and gentle.

He drew her up, taking her in his arms, so that she became small and nestling. She began to melt, small and wonderful, aware of her own softness now as his hands moved over her with swan-like caresses.

He led her to the bed where they'd lain so many times before. He laid her down gently, then stood back, admiring the silly, beautiful shape of her. She reached for him, feeling slow and peaceful, a calm sea. He came to her, lay beside her, his caresses languid and his gaze never leaving her. She opened herself to his skilled, tender touch, and there was beauty in her breast and she was now more than the roll of wave. Stronger, fuller the sensations flowed, a billowing, rolling rhythm, plunging her deep. She was submerged beneath his touch, sweet flesh. Her breath tasted of pleasure. Diving deep, she let him take her to where there was no breath, no light, no weight, no more than darkness and movement and warmth. Deeper and deeper still into the very depths of her as if she were rolling away from herself. Now all was unknown, unnecessary, unimaginable. Breath was gone, being was gone. A sudden shuddering, complete convulsion, and she was gone, was no more, but was. New, reborn. Woman.

She lay in the ebb, still so far from the shore, felt

Julius's large hand curve at the nape of her neck, bringing her to his breast. His other hand rested gently, possessively on the marvelous swell of her belly. He kissed her brow. She stroked the sleek length of him, the wonder of him still awake inside her, the utter stillness of flesh beneath her fingers lovely, strong, yet sensitive, almost frail.

He held her close. She clung to him in the utter silence, becoming unknowing again except that she was on his breast, perfect, the self touched everywhere still quivering. Her caresses, learned from his own hands, could no longer be content. She heard his base groans and had never been more beautiful.

His mouth came down heavily on hers. She murmured, "Beautiful," against his lips to the fathomless feeling as he yielded with a fierce storm, joining her in a world newly formed and all at its most elemental.

Awareness of the outside came abruptly in the ring of the telephone. She moaned, nestling her face against his neck.

"Let it go," he said.

She rolled onto her back, smiling at the very sight of her, struck by her still flush beauty. "No. It's the Aunties. If I don't answer, they'll be down here with the militia ready to take me back."

"Then let me get it." He rolled off the bed. She lazily watched him go, still so warm and half-sleepy, she couldn't rouse herself to protest.

He brought the receiver to her. She lifted her eyes, questioning, and he nodded, affirming her original guess. She propped herself on one elbow. She heard Aunt Eve's voice as she pressed the receiver to her ear.

"...won't listen to reason, but if you talk to her, she might—"

"Hello, Aunt Eve." The contentment inside Lorna came into her voice, so complete even Aunt Eve was silenced for a second.

But only for a second. "Lorna, come home."

Lorna rested her free hand on Julius's hard thigh as he sat down on the bed beside her. "I am home, Aunt Eve."

"What if something happens?"

"Nothing is going to happen. I've never felt better in my life." She smiled up at Julius. "And Julius is here."

"I know." She heard the displeasure in her aunt's voice.

"I'll be fine," Lorna reassured her. "I'll call you in the morning."

Julius took the phone and set it on the small round table by the bed. He came back to the bed, sat, looked down at Lorna with dark, wide eyes, his hair tumbling around his shoulders, his features still and striking. She wanted to clutch him, to have him fast against her. She reached for him. He drew her soft against him, touching her hair delicately. His hands held her as if she were a flower. His silence was incomprehensible. If he left, when he left—how would she bear it now?

She pressed her forehead to his shoulder, clinging to him, holding him. He rested his cheek against her crown, his hands soothing her as they stroked her sides, her back, her shoulder.

"You will stay? Until the baby is born?" She had promised not to ask forever.

"Of course, I'll stay until the child comes and you are strong again."

She had promised not to ask for more. Still the longing must have shown in her eyes.

His own eyes went dark, gentle. He touched her cheek. "This is your home, Lorna. It will be your child's home. One day you'll marry once more—"

She shook her head. He smiled, always amused by her stubbornness.

"I'll not."

"Still your child will grow up here, go to school, make friends. I know what it's like to be on the outside. So do you. It is where I will always be. It is where I have belonged since the day I put my hands around another man's neck. But you, your child don't deserve to be there. You have no sins."

"I don't care for myself."

"But the child?"

She was silent. She knew how painful, how lonely it could be not to be accepted.

"We won't speak of it anymore. You'll sleep now."

Lorna studied his face with her eyes, with her fingers, knowing that, past the hard planes, the devil-may-care smile cultivated to conceal, there was a wealth of pain. Pain that she had been able to lessen but could not release him from totally. Yet her love was so strong, so complete, so utter. She had given him everything of her self. What more could she give him to bring him peace? Was there anything?

He pressed her face to his strong shoulder, caressing her hair. "Rest now. I'll go to the kitchen, find us something for dinner."

"No." She couldn't bear him to leave. She curled against him, her arms about him. She couldn't stop her plea. "Stay. Stay."

"Shh." He relaxed in her embrace, soothed her with his caresses. "I'm here."

She eased her grip. She lay on the bed beside him, felt his kiss on her cheek. She looked up at him, so dark and soft and unbearably beautiful, and felt herself happy and saddened by the touch of his lips, a kiss that would one day be goodbye.

She dropped her head to his chest. What more could she give him? There was no answer. Only outside, the sounds of a strong wind.

Chapter Fourteen

She woke in the dark. She had turned in her sleep, but the curve of Julius, the warmth of his breath was at her back, and she was comforted. *He's still here,* the thought irrational but necessary to her.

She eased herself out of the bed, no small feat, considering her advanced stage. She stood, stretched, felt the lovely heaviness of her breasts, the strong cradle of her torso. She walked to the bathroom, heard the wind outside moaning, sad. It would rain.

A queasiness came to her stomach. She rubbed her belly. "A little late for morning sickness, fella." She walked on, stopped, putting her hand to the wall as the nausea came again, stronger. "Ah, you love to torture your mother already, child?"

The wave of sickness passed. "No one has morning sickness in their ninth month," she muttered, moving again to the bathroom. "Or in this case, midnight sickness." A cramp in her belly answered her. She went still, breathing deeply, her arms rounding the weight of her stomach, supporting it with her palms. She felt pressure in her bowels and, as the pain subsided, started toward the bathroom once more.

JULIUS AWOKE, and seeing she was gone, got up. He went toward the bathroom and saw the closed door. He tapped on the door. "I'll make us some eggs, huh?"

"I—" He heard the sound of retching.

"Lorna." He twisted the doorknob, found her over the toilet. "Are you all right?"

She rested her brow on her forearms, nodded.

"You're not in…?"

She lifted her head, shook it. "No, this isn't labor, believe me. I've got some kind of stomach bug or something. Probably a twenty-four-hour thing. I've only got nineteen hours to go."

"It could be labor."

She shook her head. "No, there's no labor pains. Only a sick stomach. Diarrhea. Vomiting. It's a bug."

"Maybe it's the start of labor."

"Not according to what the books say. Besides, first babies are usually late, not early. My due date is three weeks away. My water hasn't broke and, oh no—" Embarrassed, she waved at him to leave. He left the door open a crack and stepped out into the hall. He heard her groan. He paced the narrow hall-way. Finally she emerged, wan and tired looking.

"We'd better get you to the hospital."

She shook her head. "I'm too tired. I've been up half the night. It's just the flu, I'm telling you. This isn't labor."

"How do you know? You ever been in labor before?"

"Have you?"

He studied her. "I'm taking you to the hospital."

"I'm too tired to put my shoes on, let alone give birth."

"I'll put your shoes on."

She started down the hall. "Just let me go back to bed. It's only a stomach virus. I'll be fine as soon as it passes."

"Are you sure?"

She had almost reached the bedroom. She nodded. "Believe me, I've read as much about pregnancy and childbirth as I did farming, and nowhere does it say it includes diarrhea and vomiting. This is a bug." She waved her hand, dismissing any further discussion, and disappeared into the bedroom.

Julius stood in the hall, uncertain. He moved to the bedroom, stood in the doorway. She had crawled beneath the covers and lay curled on her side, her eyes closed, her breaths even as if already asleep. He went over to the bed, laid a hand on her shoulder.

"Lorna?" He jiggled her shoulder.

"What?" she murmured, her eyes staying closed.

"What could it hurt to go to the hospital?"

"I'm too tired to get up out of this bed, let alone get dressed. It's a bug. It'll pass."

So stubborn. He stroked her pale cheek, feeling helpless, sitting there doing nothing. He heard the strong wind outside. He knew nothing about childbirth. The only other pregnant person he'd ever known was his sister. His gaze went to the medal around Lorna's neck.

He stood and lifted Lorna into his arms, blankets and all.

"What the hell—" Her eyes opened and glared at him.

"We're going to the hospital."

"I told you—"

"I don't care what you told me. We're not taking any chances."

"I'm not even dressed. I've only got a robe on beneath these blankets.

"You'd only undress at the hospital. Now you're one step ahead of the game."

"I told you I'm not—whoa."

She gasped hard, went so stiff in his arms he stopped. He stared down at her, frightened.

Her breath came back. She looked up at him. "What're you doing standing around? Get me to the hospital."

He went to the front door. Lorna twisted the knob.

He kicked open the door. Another pain came as he walked down the steps. Her fingers clutched his arm. "Stop, stop," she cried. He went motionless. She panted. Finally her breath eased.

"Maybe we should call—"

Her fingernails dug into his arm. "Hurry."

He moved, panic building with each step. No, not again. He wouldn't lose anyone else he loved. "I've got you," he told her, concealing his own fear. He chose her car over his truck so she could lie down across the back seat. He'd forgotten the car keys. He ran back in, searching until he found them thrown on her bedroom dresser. He ran back out, jumped into the car, slammed it into reverse, heard her moan. His heart wrenched.

"Hang on, honey. We're on our way."

He pulled onto the road. There was only the sound of Lorna's pants punctuated by groans. With each moan, he pressed his foot harder on the gas pedal.

"Hang on, hang on," he muttered as if the words were magic.

He heard a gasp.

"My water just broke."

"Oh, hell." They were still at the stretch of open road empty of houses. The speedometer needle jumped.

"There's pressure, a lot of pressure."

"Don't push." He remembered that much from television. "Don't push."

She was panting, gasping. "I can feel him. The baby, the baby's coming."

"That's impossible," Julius yelled.

"Tell him that," she screamed from the back seat. She released a long wail. "Julius, stop the car. Pull over. Pull over." She was screeching like a madwoman.

"We've got to get you to the hospital."

"The baby's coming now." Her screams were like the fierce swirl of the wind.

He swung to the side of the road, jumped out, yanked open the car's back door. She was propped up on her elbows, knees pulled up, the blankets tented over her legs. He saw the dark stain of her waters on the seat, pulled back the covers, revealing her opened thighs. He stared at a dark crown pressing between her legs. He'd never been more frightened or fascinated in his life.

He looked up, seeing her fear, and pushed his own aside. He looked around, saw the nearest house about a quarter mile down the road. He looked back at her.

"Don't leave me, Julius. Stay."

He nodded. "I won't leave you, Lorna. Don't worry. I'll be right here. Right here." He took a breath.

"Don't let anything happen to the baby, Julius."

"Don't you worry. I'm not going to let anything happen to you or this baby. You know how many calves I've helped bring into this world in my lifetime?'' He wasn't going to tell her only one. ''Most natural thing in the world.''

She emitted another low wail. When it subsided, he continued soothingly, ''Why, you've got the hard part, darling. All I've got to do is sit down here and catch him when he pops out. No harder than a game of Sunday softball.''

She mustered a wan smile. He looked at her face and vowed nothing would happen to this woman or her child. He would deliver this baby.

''Okay, honey, let's have a baby. The next time you feel like you have to push, go ahead.''

She curled upward, gritting her teeth and bore down until she collapsed onto her back, panting. He waited until her heavy breaths lessened.

''Okay, again, push.''

The dark crown pressed, Lorna's body widened.

''Once more,'' he instructed after Lorna caught her breath. ''Hard.'' She leaned up once more. Julius counted to ten, not letting her stop pushing until he was done.

''Once more.''

''I can't.''

''You can.''

She gritted her teeth and, with a force he didn't know she had left, curled upward and bore down.

''It's coming, it's coming.'' He eased his hands around the tiny head, gently twisting it upward until he saw the cord around the baby's neck.

"Wait! Wait!"

"What is it?" Lorna leaned up, trying to see.

"The cord."

"Oh God, save my baby, Julius. Save my baby."

Carefully Julius pulled on the cord until it slackened and eased it over the child's head. "It's off."

"It's okay? He's okay? I don't hear anything. Why don't I hear anything?"

Julius saw the child's stillness, the blue color blending with the blood and fluids.

"No!" His defiance split the night. He rapped the baby on the back once, twice, three times. No response. He lay the tiny infant on Lorna's stomach, heaving with her sobs. He tenderly tilted the baby's small, slick head. The boy's chin lifted, and Julius saw the child's mother in that already strong angle. He would save this baby. He bowed his head and blew his own life into the child. Several small pushes to the chest, then again his breath became the child's as if he were no more than life himself. Again, delicate pushes to the chest.

"Breathe. Breathe." He chanted like a madman now. His breath pushed into the child, warm, moist, filling him. He massaged the chest. Lorna touched his crown.

"Make him breathe." He didn't know to whom he prayed, only that he prayed. "Make him breathe."

The tiny body started, the limbs jumping as if jolted. He turned the child on its stomach, hitting his back once more. The body twitched again, fluid covered Lorna's stomach and a cry filled the air and became one with the wind whirling all around.

Lorna's sobs were silent now as he gently placed the infant in her arms, careful of the cord still attached and covered them both with the dry end of the blanket. He touched the child's delicate crown, blood-streaked and beautiful. Lorna reached for his hand, brought it to her cheek to kiss its palm. "Thank you, thank you."

He kissed her brow, the top of the baby's head, so overcome with exhaustion and the enormity of it all, he couldn't speak. He secured them in the back seat and got behind the wheel to get them to the hospital. He stared for a dazed moment at his hands clutching the steering wheel. Hands that in the past had taken a life now had saved a life. Not only the child's but his own. He dropped his forehead to those hands and gave grace. He had been delivered.

LORNA SANK into the propped pillows at her back. She felt weary and wonderful with the strength of a hundred men, with the deep, new calm of a woman who had given birth. She saw her child cradled in his grandfather's arms, the picture as natural as the life process itself.

Axel smiled down at his grandson. "Hey, Boss," he murmured, rocking the infant, a rare happiness revealed on his features.

Lorna smiled, remembering her vow never to call any man "the Boss" again. She looked at her son, this six pounds, twelve ounces of miracle, and knew her vow had been broken months ago. This child had been the boss since the beginning. Not that she would ever call him that to his face. To his face, he would be called Nicholas. But in her heart, the child would always be "the Boss."

One vow broken without regret. Maybe one day, she would even marry again. She looked at the life cradled in her father's arms. Anything was possible. She knew that now.

The Aunties hovered on either side of the child, but Axel wouldn't relinquish his hold. Aunt Eve held out a finger, laughed as the infant's fingers, no longer than an inch, wrapped around hers.

"O-o-oh my, such a strong, firm grip."

Axel nodded. "Of course. He's a McDonough. You're tough, aren't you, Boss?"

Birdy stepped away from the others and moved to Lorna's side. "How you doing, mommy?" She brushed the hair off her niece's forehead.

"It happened so fast, it still doesn't seem real. I'm not complaining though, after some of the labor stories I've heard. I only had a little pain and that was at the end. Shoot." She laughed. "I thought it was the flu."

Her father glanced at her. "Your mother gave birth the same way. Remember, Eve?"

Eve nodded. "If I hadn't gotten her off the toilet, she would've had you right there."

"She had such an easy time of it, she was like you, laughing about it. And then..." The shadows came back to her father's face. He leaned down and kissed the child's forehead.

"Okay, you've hogged him long enough." Eve reached out her arms. "My turn." She took the baby from her brother and sat down in the chair beside the bed, cooing to the child.

Axel's hands stayed lifted as if not knowing where to go now that they were empty. He looked at his daughter. She smiled at him, a parent now too, who would also make mistakes along the way no matter how much she loved her child.

Her father's gaze returned to the child, then came back to Lorna. He nodded, something in his eyes she'd never seen before. Happiness.

"You did good, Lorna. I'm proud of you."

"Thank you...Daddy." It was a beginning. It may be as close as they'd ever come. All Lorna knew was, in that moment, it all seemed so easy.

Past her father, she saw Julius standing at the opened door. She smiled at him.

He stood at the room's entrance, unable to move. He had never seen her more beautiful—her hair fanned out across the pillows, tumbled across her shoulders. Weariness darkened her skin but joy shone in her eyes, seemed to glow about her. He felt the same glow, the same triumph of life within him. He looked and saw its victory snuggled right now in an Auntie's arms.

Axel turned in the direction of his daughter's smile. Julius nodded, his expression guarded. Axel considered him gravely.

"There he is," Birdy chimed. "The man of the hour. I'm calling the paper today and make sure they get your picture and the whole story for tomorrow's edition."

Julius shook his head. "No, ma'am, that's not necessary."

"Nonsense," Eve retorted. "About time that rag printed some good news for a change. Do this community good to read a happy story when it happens." She looked down at the child. "Right, Nicholas?"

Julius heard the name. He looked at Lorna. She touched the gold medal always around her throat now.

"Julius?" Lorna's father cleared his throat and stepped toward the man. His expression gruff, he offered his hand.

Julius looked at the outstretched hand, then met it with his own.

"Thank you." Axel's manner was brusque, but he didn't let go of Julius's hand. "If there's any way I can repay you. Anything you need."

Lorna looked at the two men's clasped hands and

knew her father had just given Julius everything he needed.

"Thank you," Axel said again. He released Julius.

"C'mon, Eve, Bernadette, I need a cup of that swill they pass off as coffee around here." Her father's voice was still strangely rough.

Aunt Birdy went to Julius. "You're a good boy." Standing on tiptoe, she kissed him on the cheek. Lorna smiled as he reddened.

Eve stood and offered the child to Julius. "Here you go, Nicholas. You know this guy, don't you?" Julius awkwardly took the baby. Eve patted his arm, then impulsively wrapped her arms around him and the baby and gave them both a hug.

"Do you two want anything?" Axel asked from the doorway as he waited for his sister.

Julius and Lorna shook their heads.

"I'm bringing them back a piece of pie anyway," Eve said as she joined her brother and sister.

"Lorna would rather have chocolate cake. It's her favorite," Birdy insisted.

"She hasn't eaten chocolate since she was a child. You must be going senile, sister."

"Well, if I am, then we'll finally have something in common."

The Aunties' voices faded as Lorna and Julius softly laughed. Lorna didn't speak for a moment, enjoying the sight of her son and Julius. "You're still blushing," she teased.

"Yeah, well..." He sat down in the chair beside the bed, cradling the baby.

"Not used to all this admiration?"

He arched a brow. She smiled. "I wouldn't be surprised if my father had a statue erected to you in the center of the town square."

"Beats him wanting to hang me in the center of the town square." Julius traced the baby's cheek with his gentle touch.

"Are you going right back to the farm after you leave here?" he asked, his attention still in the crib.

"Yes. The Aunties offered to come out for a few weeks and help out."

"That's good. Good you'll have help. I hear the first few weeks after birth can be rough."

"Stick around and see for yourself." She kept her voice casual, but her heart was pounding as he met her eyes.

In those gray-green eyes, Julius saw the questions, need, desire. He looked at the child, so small and miraculous, nothing but possibility.

Like the seeds Lorna and he had sown together in the soil, in their hearts. Seeds that would grow and bloom if nurtured, respected, loved. He lifted his eyes to Lorna again. He saw the hope. He reached for her hand.

"When do we go home?" he asked her. Now her eyes held happiness. She lifted his hand, pressed it to her heart. He leaned over and kissed her deeply.

"I love you, Lorna."

"I love you, Julius."

His hand still held hers. The infant in his arm had found his finger, wrapped his hand around it as if to never let go. He looked down at his hands, joined with the woman and child who had changed his life, taught him to love again and be loved. His hands tightened and hung on. He would never let go.

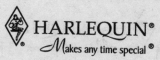

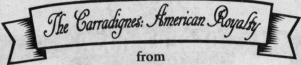

If you enjoyed what you just read,
then we've got an offer you can't resist!

Take 2 bestselling
love stories FREE!
Plus get a FREE surprise gift!

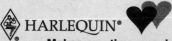